Kristina, 1904:

The "Greenhorn Girl"

Elizabeth Claire

Illustrations by
Len Shalansky

Copy Editors: Nadine Simms, Adelaide Coles, Nancy Baxer, Warren Murphy, and Marilyn Gelman

Illustrations: Len Shalansky

Saddle Brook, NJ, 07663 USA
Printed in the United States of America

ISBN: 978-0-937630-21-1

Kristina, 1904: The Greenhorn Girl

For today's new immigrants,
and for the memory of my grandmother,
Elizabeth Klimek

Acknowledgements

I am grateful that my grandmother, at the age of 95, was able to read the early version of this collection of her stories a couple of decades ago. Thanks to her, it was my good fortune to be born in the U.S., and she often would remind me of the luxury I enjoyed compared to the hardships of "the old days," and "the old country."

Thanks to writing mentor Warren Murphy for his encouragement in this project from those earliest days. I deeply appreciate all those who have contributed to the work, including Barry Moreno, librarian at the Ellis Island Monument for his painstaking reading and correcting of the text and the illustrations for historical accuracy. Thanks to Len Shalansky for his patience and meticulous execution of detail in his illustrations, and to Dave Nicholson for last minute art consultations and editing.

Thanks to Nancy Baxer for early readings and constant encouragement, to Nadine Simms for eagle-eyed copy editing, and to Adelaide Coles for knowing the heart of a teen-age girl. The Materials Writers' Special Interst group of International TESOL furnished support and advice including Lynda Steyne with important Slovak details and translations. Thanks to Tina DiBella and Fumie Fukushima for careful reading of the manuscript, and to Marilyn Gelman and Devra Weingart for support and pointers.

Kristina, 1904: The Greenhorn Girl

Contents

Kristina, 1904: The Greenhorn Girl

Foreword

Between 1880 and 1914, at least 7.5 million people from Eastern Europe migrated to the U.S. These immigrants were part of what is known as the "second great wave" of American immigration, driven by poverty and hunger in Eastern Europe, and drawn by hopes of jobs, and the promise of freedom from the stifling rule of autocratic governments back home. The port of entry for all immigrants was Castle Garden in Manhattan (1855-1890) and later, Ellis Island (1892-1954).

The story of *Kristina, 1904: The "Greenhorn Girl"* details the human side of this historical migration. The episodes are based on true stories that I heard while growing up from my grandmother and her sisters. Their recounting of the traumas and costs of the trip to America, and the difficulties, embarrassments, and exploitation they experienced during their first years here left a lasting impression. Often the stories began with the introduction, "You don't know how lucky you are." As a child, I was always fascinated by the poignant drama of the stories, and by high school, I realized I was hearing history, illuminating the dry data in my social studies book.

I began to pay closer attention, and recorded my grandmother's words. And as I later researched the details of life for immigrants in the early 1900s, I came to truly appreciate how lucky I am that such courage existed in my family—and in yours.

The power of my grandmother's stories helped me choose my career as an ESL teacher, joyfully inspired to help today's courageous newcomers feel welcome, to learn English, and learn how to survive in their new environment. These most recent newcomers are part of America now, and their stories of the difficult early days will be told years from now and live on with their own grandchildren.

Chapter 1: Saying Goodbye

When the white rooster crowed at the first light of dawn, fourteen-year-old Kristina Surinova's eyes snapped open. She stretched her arms straight up so as not to bump into her still sleeping younger sister Olga. Opening her eyes wide to let in as much light as possible, she looked around the large room that was sleeping quarters for her family at night, living room and cobbler shop by day. Was it possible to press the scene so firmly in her memory that she could make a permanent picture of her home, and carry it with her for the rest of her life? She knew she was never going to see it again.

She and ten-year old Olga were lying in a large straw bed with a puffy goose-down quilt; next to it was the trundle bed with twelve-year old Anna and eight-year-old Betka, and in the corner was the crib with sleeping Susanna, five years old, curled up into a ball because she had kicked her covers off. The walls were hung with shoemaker's leather, cutting tools, and half-finished boots and purses. Kristina pressed this picture into her mind.

Two windows let in the early rays of sun. Kristina picked herself out of the warmth of the goose down, shivered in her long night dress, bent over the crib to replace the covers on little Susanna, and tickled her ribs at the same time. She didn't wait for them to wake, but slipped out of bed to begin her morning chores.

She pulled on her shawl, stepped into leather slippers, gathered the wooden bucket from the tin sink, and opened the creaking door and went out to fetch water for the morning's breakfast. As Kristina passed the white rooster on her way to the brook he squawked and flew out of her path to join his half dozen wives. "Goodbye chickens," Kristina said briskly, firmly storing the picture of them scratching and pecking for bugs and seeds in the bare patches of ground. Two geese, still looking slightly naked from their spring plucking, honked in complaint as Kristina passed without offering them anything to eat. "Goodbye geese," she said.

She lowered the heavy wooden bucket into the cold waters of the well behind their two-room white

cement house. The bucket came up splashing, filled with sparkling, icy cold water. It was heavy, and some spilled on her bare legs, making a shiver run down her spine. Nine days from today, and she would be in the land of water-from-the-faucet, right-into-the-sink. Hot water, it would be, too, Mother had written. That would be in the great, the golden, the gorgeous full-of-food place: New York City. Today, May 21, 1904 would be her last day to be hungry, to see her sisters hungry, and to be helpless to do anything about it.

She was going to America.

Over the past three weeks, there had been the dizzying excitement of preparations and the soon-to-be-fulfilled longing to see her mother again. The excitement had alternated with the dread of the nine-day land and sea trip and the sorrow of leaving her sisters, her home, and everything familiar to her. She knew she would miss her sisters terribly. But she wondered if she would miss her father and his gruff voice and the leather belt he used so often on her legs. *Would she be yelled at and strapped for mistakes in America?*

And would Father miss her?

At this thought, she looked up and saw him coming up the dirt road from the town, carrying the marketing basket. He pushed the leaning wooden gate open with his knee and walked into the yard.

"I have some things for your trip. Come, pack them. The wagon will be here soon." His voice was commanding and gruff as always. *Would he not show any softness toward her even today, the last day she would ever see him? Wasn't he sorry she was leaving? Wasn't he going to have to teach Anna to keep the house and cook? Would that make him miss her?*

Kristina dared to look at his eyes, trying to understand the mystery of her father. But today his face was the same embittered stone it had become when Mother had left for America two years before.

Father walked quickly into the small alcove that served as a kitchen, and his eyes took in the still sprawling girls in the beds.

"Anna! Olga! Betka! Susanna! You're not dressed yet?" Father's voice could flog as well as the leather strap he used so often. "The beds are not made! Kristina's chores are yours now. Susanna, feed the chickens and geese, and see if there are eggs for breakfast. Betka, go to the brook. Bring the milk and the goose fat. Olga, take care of the bedding. Anna, fix breakfast."

Couldn't he be kind, just once on this last day?

The four younger girls—Anna, Betka, Olga, and Susanna—suddenly came to life. Fingers flew on buttons, as each girl helped another to do the row of fasteners down the back of their long brown dresses. Aprons were tied. The covers were carefully hauled off the beds and taken outside to hang on the fence.

Father placed the grocery basket on the table. "Get a large cloth. Wrap these," he said. The aroma told Kristina the contents of the basket before she saw it: salami. A heavenly, garlic-full salami. She breathed in deeply with surprise and pleasure. Father placed the salami on the white linen napkin Kristina had spread on the table. She handed him the knife and he cut the entire length of the red-brown cylinder into thick, quarter-inch slices. She waited for him to remove half of the mouth-watering meat to keep at home.

He shook his head. "It's a long trip to America—a half day to Vienna, two days on the train to Hamburg. Seven days across the ocean to New York." He lifted two fresh, crusty loaves of rye bread from the basket. Kristina could hardly believe it. Two loaves of baker's bread and a whole salami just for her!

"Thank you, Father," she said.

"There'll be food on the ship. But you won't like it much, from what I hear," Father added.

"Soon I'll be sending you money from America so you can have salami whenever you want it," said Kristina, hoping to reassure her father that this expense on her behalf would not be forgotten.

"Maybe," said Father, "maybe not."

How could there be any question? In America a person could work and buy food and there'd be something left over. The money that Mother sent to them was proof. It had fed them for the two dreadful years that she had been gone. But Kristina and her sisters were growing, there were fewer and fewer customers for Father's shoes, and now even with the money from America, it was no longer enough to feed six people. The family needed another wage earner. They had saved for a year, and now there was enough: forty dollars. It had bought passage for Kristina on a ship to America.

"May I . . . " Kristina looked at her father, then hesitated. Father guarded every morsel of food with an iron ferocity, doling it out at meals with precision, seeing none was ever wasted, and seeing that none of them ever got a crumb more than they needed to keep from fainting. But as today was her last day, and with the generosity of the salami, Kristina dared: "May I . . .take some pickles, too?"

The wooden keg in the corner held very few from last season's garden, and it would be months before this year's crop was ready.

"Yes. Take some pickles. Take five."

"Five! Thank you, Father!" Today was a miracle. Kristina triumphantly scooped five beauties from of the barrel in the kitchen and wrapped them, dripping, in brown paper. She placed the pickles with the bread and salami and carefully tied up the corners of the linen napkin around them. Then she and her sister Anna prepared breakfast.

It did not take long to cook, and even less time to eat. Two hens' eggs and a goose egg soft-boiled and divided among six people made only a spoonful on each plate. Father measured out goose fat and Anna spread it on six slices of yesterday's bread. Susanna and Olga had milk. Kristina, Betka, and Anna drank coffee, as Father did.

"Tinka, you're so lucky!" said Olga for the hundredth time this week. With a mouth still full of bread, continued, "You're going to live with Mother!"

"Not exactly," said Kristina, repeating patiently to the ten-year-old. "I'm going to live with a family and be their maid."

"But you'll be in the same city as Mother," insisted Olga. "You'll see her on your days off. Every week! That's better than we have."

"Yes," answered Kristina. "But I won't have my sisters! I'm going to miss you very much!"

They were right to be jealous, Kristina thought—she would escape the beatings of their father and be near their gentle mother. Good, strong, smiling Mother, whose warmth and touch she and her sisters all had longed for, seemingly all their lives.

The first time Mother had gone away to work had only been as far as Vienna—a day's trip away. She had left Kristina, Anna, Olga, and Betka in the care of Babka, their ancient great-grandmother. Kristina had been seven years old then. Mother's visits home were never long enough for them: a week every three months. After Susanna was born, though, Mother had stayed home a whole year before going off again; a year later, when the last baby, Milka, was born, they had Mother for another year. The times that Mother was home the little house sang with delights, with home-baked bread, with stories read before bedtime, being tucked in and kissed. And when she went away, life was dreary, gray, and unbearable. Two years ago, Mother had gone to America. For these awful past two years, there had been a half continent and a whole ocean separating them . . . and the impossible barrier of the forty-dollar ticket.

During those years, for his part, Father had hunched over his cobbler's table on one side of the room, all day and into the night, cutting and sewing leather, and hammering wooden heels on the shoes he was making. In the evenings he demanded silence as Babka read the Bible to the girls and taught them long prayers and hymns. Father frightened the girls with stories of hellish punishments for breaking any of his rules, and especially if they dared asked for more to eat. Once, when Olga had dared to ask for a little bread before going to sleep, he smacked her across the face and thundered, "God is sleeping in the bread!" So none of them ever asked again.

When the letters from America arrived with money in them, they had more food in their bellies, and things began to seem bearable for a while.

Babka had gotten chilled in the winter, had taken sick for a month and died, but it did not bring Mother home. Kristina had been half-way through the sixth grade at school when Father decided she should leave so she could keep house and take over the duties of mothering her five sisters. Father, who had completely given up smiling and whose face became permanently etched with bitterness, impatiently taught her to bake bread, make soup and noodles, shop in the market, keep house, and wash the family's clothing in the icy waters behind their house. His lessons were always punctuated with criticisms and sudden smacks for her mistakes. And there was the belt.

The cholera epidemic had struck the summer after Babka died. All six girls had gotten sick one after another, and there had been no money for a doctor. The neighbors said that the doctors weren't doing any good for the cholera anyway. The younger ones cried for Mother; Kristina, feverish herself, had held them and prepared soups and liquids for them as best she could. Baby Milka had the fever the worst; she whimpered for days, becoming weaker and weaker as she could not hold any food in her body for long. One miserable day, Kristina herself was too weak to walk around, and just sat holding Milka in her arms, rocking, rocking in the large wooden chair, trying to get her to drink water to cool her burning little body. And then Milka just stopped breathing. Kristina cuddled her, tickled her, patted her, but to no avail. Kristina had screamed, and it hurt her throat, and she couldn't talk for quite a while after that.

They had buried Milka in the church yard next to the four brothers Kristina had never known. They had all died from one disease or another before Kristina had been born. "The neighbors had a name for their sickness," Mother had told her, "but it was the hunger, the hunger that they really died of."

"Quickly now," barked Father. "Clean up. The wagon will be here any minute. I'm going to work outside. I'll call you when it comes. Check your bundle to see if you have everything."

The other girls took their dishes to the washstand and scampered out to watch for the wagon, leaving Kristina alone. Staring into the small speckled mirror that hung in the kitchen she brushed her long brown wavy hair and pinned the pink ribbon in it that Betka had given her

as a goodbye present. Kristina glanced toward the door to be sure Father was not watching—he said looking in the mirror was vanity, a deadly sin—then she leaned closer to examine her hazel eyes, her round and slightly turned up nose, her small mouth with straight white teeth. She was satisfied—the neighbors said she was beginning to look more and more like Mother, and that pleased her. To Kristina, Mother was the most beautiful woman in the world.

Kristina swung her traveling bundle onto the straw bed, undid the knots in the coarse cotton blanket, laid the blanket out flat, and checked the contents again. All the things she owned in the world were going with her: a second brown dress, a petticoat, two undershirts, black stockings, a comb, a brush, some soap, and a small pillow to ease the hardness of the trip as Mother had advised. It wasn't very much. But at least it wouldn't be heavy.

Kristina sat down on the bed next to the things that would accompany her to America. She patted the worn muslin sheets. Oh, the talking and giggling that had gone on in this corner of the little house! The secrets they had shared in soft whispers lest Father get out his strap to punish them for making noise after bedtime. Who would she tell her secrets to in America?

"Goodbye bed," she sighed.

"That's silly, saying goodbye to a bed!"

Kristina whirled around. She had not heard Anna come in. "It is silly," she admitted. But I'm just saying goodbye to everything I'll never see again."

"You'll have a better bed in America," said Anna.

"But no sisters to keep warm with on cold nights!"

Anna was quiet a moment, and Kristina noticed that she had her hands behind her back.

"What's in your hands?"

"It's a present for you, Tinka. A goodbye present." Anna extended a worn, dog-eared book toward Kristina.

"Oh Anna, it's your fairy tale book!"

"You'll need something to read on the ship."

"Are you sure you don't want to keep it for yourself?" Besides the huge family Bible, Anna's fairy tale book was the only book in the house.

"I know all the stories by heart," said Anna. "And I won't have time to read now anyway. I'll be busy taking care of the house." She turned away, her eyes filling with tears. "And I'll miss you, Kristina, I'll

miss you so much." She then turned again and flung her arms around Kristina and hugged her tightly. "I wish you wouldn't have to go," Anna cried. Kristina held her sister and waited until her sobbing subsided.

"I'm sorry you have to leave school, Anna," said Kristina.

"Well, you left school to take care of the house and all of us. Now it's my turn," sniffed Anna. "I don't mind it so much, I'm always getting the stick for dreaming in class and forgetting my lessons. School is wasted on me. But you really loved your studies, Kristina. You were the best in your class, always getting prizes."

"Well, that's long over now," said Kristina. "Six years of school. Father says that any more than that is a waste of time for a girl. And he didn't want us to learn all that Hungarian history and language anyhow. It's not really meant for us Slovaks, he says, and it would make us forget our own language and our own culture. He says that's what the emperor wants—to destroy our identity."

"So now I'll get a Slovak education." Anna laughed bitterly. "Like you did. Father is going to teach me how to cook and wash and take care of the house." Anna kicked the leg of the bed with the toe of her high-buttoned shoe. "If Mother cared about us, she wouldn't have left us."

"You mustn't blame Mother!" Kristina said. She

had argued this many times before with Anna. "She loves us. She went to America so she can send money to buy food for us to eat. The people in Myjava can't afford to pay much for shoes; no matter how hard Father works, it isn't enough."

"Then why didn't Father go to America instead of Mother? There are lots of people in America who need shoes. Half of our town has already gone there."

"Shh. He'll hear you," warned Kristina.

"I don't care," said Anna, but she lowered her voice to a whisper. "If Father had been the one to leave, I wouldn't miss him with his long strap and bad temper."

"Honor your mother and father, Anna," reminded Kristina. "It says so in the commandments. And anyway, you'll be the next one to come to America. It won't take long, with both Mother and me working. We'll save the forty dollars for your ticket in a year, I bet. You'll be thirteen. That's old enough, I think, to get a job like mine."

Anna shook her head. "Olga will be only eleven. She won't be able to cook and take care of the younger two. No, I think it'll be a longer time before I can escape from Father."

The three younger girls charged indoors. "The wagon is here!" shouted Betka.

"Let me carry your bundles!" cried little Susanna.

"You're too little, Susanna," said Olga. "Betka and I will carry them. Olga pulled the corners of the blanket together and knotted them, and tied a second knot to make a carrying handle. She heaved the bundle over her shoulder and Betka gathered up the smaller napkin-wrapped bundle with its aromatic contents.

"Here, you can carry my book," said Kristina to Susanna.

Susanna took the book and stood still a moment. Then she suddenly dropped it and wrapped her arms around Kristina's waist, immobilizing her. Tears streamed down her cheeks, and wails came from deep in her throat. "I don't have a mother, and now I won't have my Tinka! Don't go Tinka, Don't go!"

Kristina lifted Susanna and kissed her on her forehead and cheeks. "I'll miss you too, Little One. You're my treasure, my little treasure." Tears poured down her cheeks, too.

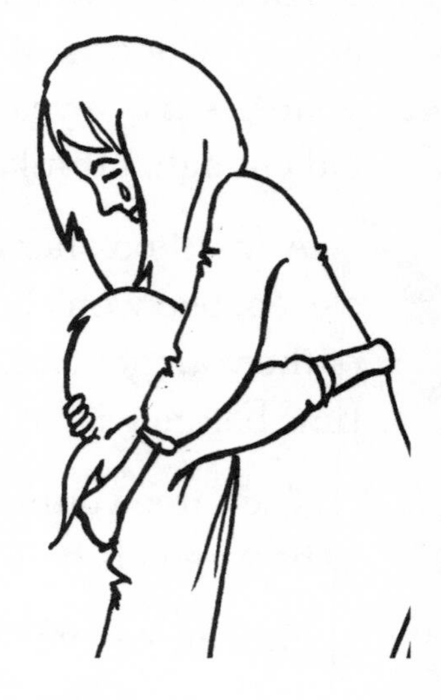

"Don't go! Don't go!" Susanna screamed, now almost choking Kristina with her grasp around her waist.

"Don't worry, we'll all be together again someday,

you'll see." Kristina tried to sound completely certain, remembering the words her mother had said two long years ago. But she was hardly convinced herself, so how could she convince Susanna?

What if Susanna should become sick like Milka? What if she died? Kristina held Susanna tightly to her and tried to drive those thoughts from her mind, but the vision of the graveyard seemed too strong. Olga, Anna and Betka threw their arms around Kristina and Susanna, and all five girls sobbed and wailed hysterically. Kristina's heart ached; she lost all of her desire to leave. She loved her little sisters and they truly needed her.

The horses stamped impatiently, raising dust in the road and the wagon driver called out, "You have a train to catch, remember!" His voice was kind but firm. He earned his living by delivering people to the railroad station, and sometimes had to bodily pull such grieving children from a parent, who could not board his wagon otherwise.

Kristina tore herself from the younger girls and Father put his hands together to form a step helping her climb up into the wagon. Pani Gregorova, their neighbor, held out her hand to Kristina and made room for her on the hard wooden bench. The wagon was now full.

Kristina knew them all: Pan Novak, the cheese

maker, Pan Vlecor, a woodcutter, Pani Vlecorova, his wife, and Pani Strcek, the tanner's wife.

"Good morning, Pani Surinova," they said, greeting Kristina with the title of respect due an adult now that she was going to be a wage earner.

"Good morning," she managed, not embarrassed by her tears, and not able to take her eyes away from her sisters. Father climbed up in front of the wagon to sit with the driver. He would go with them as far as the train station.

Olga's and Betka's faces were contorted with

sobs as they handed up Kristina's two bundles. Anna looked stunned, and held onto Susanna. Kristina leaned out over the side, reaching to touch her sisters' hands. The driver clicked to the horses, slapped the reins lightly on their backs and the heavily loaded wagon began to creak on its way.

The four younger girls walked along-side the wagon, taking turns holding Kristina's hand. As the wagon picked up speed, they jogged to keep up with it.

"Write to us, Kristina!"

"Tell us about America!"

"Send a picture if you can!"

"Give Mother kisses from us!"

Susanna's legs gave out first and she could no longer keep up with the wagon. "Don't go! Don't go! Don't go!" she screamed again and again.

Soon Olga, then Betka, and finally Anna, became exhausted and had to let the wagon go on without them.

Chapter 2: On the Train

Pani Gregorova's eyes were as red and wet as Kristina's own. She squeezed Kristina close to her and sighed a long sigh. "Ah, your poor sisters, your poor sisters. My own children cried so hard, too." She sobbed for a few moments, then blew her nose and dried her cheeks. "We have no choice. When our families are hungry, we do what we must do."

Pani Gregorova was to be Kristina's guardian on the trip to America, since a young girl was not allowed to travel alone. "Do you have the purse I made for you to wear around your neck?" she asked.

Kristina nodded and patted her chest.

"Birth certificate, traveling documents?"

"Yes."

"And your ticket?"

Kristina had her ticket, the key that was about to open a new door of her life.

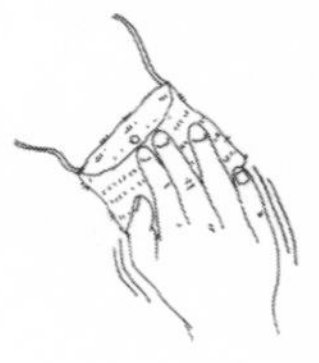

It granted her passage on the huge, mythical ship, the *Kaiser Wilhelm der Grosse,* the very same ship Mother had sailed to America on. A family of six in Myjava could live for a month on the cost of one ticket. It had taken Mother a year to save the unimaginable amount of forty dollars to bring Kristina to America.

The road, filled with rocks and bumps followed the winding brook that flowed through the village of Myjava. Each turn of the large wooden wheels jostled Kristina's spine on the hard wooden bench. She had seldom been out of her own small village before, and gradually her interest and curiosity in the new sights conquered her sadness. The road led through woods, then through another village like her own. Here, the brook was joined by another, forming a full river; women stood knee deep in the water, pounding white as snow sheets on wooden slabs. The wagoner stopped to let the horses drink before continuing over a rackety wooden bridge. As in Myjava, a church faced one end of a large grassy square; neat lines of whitewashed houses formed a border for the single dirt road through the village. Some people waved, calling out "Good luck! Find lots of gold!" The villagers knew that wagons full of people and the blanket-wrapped bundles were going to the railroad, and ultimately destined for America.

Kristina thought she would not miss this land, this poor land that had never been independent, and that had even lost its own name. The

Hungarians who were the most recent overlords did not allow the Slovaks to call their land Slovakia anymore. Hungarian soldiers patrolled the streets; the public schools were taught by Hungarians; Hungarians owned the stores; Hungarians made the rules. If hunger were not enough reason, the desire for freedom created another powerful urge that pulled the Slovaks out of their own land.

Once, when her Sunday school group had had a picnic in the woods and were singing Slovak songs, the Hungarian soldiers shot into the air to warn them that they mustn't sing so near the village. The Hungarian teachers in the school told all the children how proud they should be to be a part of the Great Austro-Hungarian Empire. The Slovak children merely nodded and thought their own private thoughts.

Conversation picked up in the wagon. "Where in America are you going?" Pani Strcek asked Pani Gregorova.

"My husband is in Little Falls, in New York. He says I can get work there in a place that makes cheese. And you, where?"

"I am going to Pennsylvania to join my husband. There are many Slovaks there working in the coal mines. My husband has been there for three years, saving up for me to come. We'll rent a big house and then we can take in boarders, coal miners who are not married, or whose wives have not arrived yet. They'll pay us rent and board; I'll cook for them and wash their clothes. This way, we can make ends meet and have some to save to bring the children to be with us.

"It will be a better life for us all," announced Pan Vlecor. "In America, no one has to go hungry if he's willing to work hard."

"And there are no soldiers to keep you from gathering with your friends on the street, or from singing your own songs," added Pan Melc.

"You mean people from Slovakia can sing Slovak songs in the streets of America?" asked Kristina, amazed.

"Don't you know? America is a free country," said Pan Vlecor. "They have a democracy."

"What's that?"

"The people are the ones who elect the leaders When young men become twenty-one, if they are citizens, they can vote. They choose a president to be the leader for four years. No one rules for a lifetime like an emperor."

Kristina pondered that amazing thought for quite a while.

"You seem very small to be going to America," said Pani Strcek to Kristina. "Can you do a day's work?"

"I'm fourteen. I've done the cooking and cleaning

since my Babka died. Father taught me. I take care of my sisters and wash the clothes too." She didn't add that she thought that working for a rich family in America would be much easier than working in her own home. Rich people would have water in pipes, inside their houses, and hot water besides. No more hauling heavy buckets from the stream. She wouldn't have to wash clothing in a frozen brook anymore, breaking the ice to scrub her sisters' blouses and her father's shirts. No rich person could be as demanding as Father, who wanted his shirts as white as the snow, and never mind the frozen fingers. Mother had written that Kristina would have all of Thursday, and half of Sunday free to do whatever she wanted. Poor Anna. All the work of caring for the family in Myjava would be hers now.

In the early afternoon, the wagon slowed down and joined a line with other wagons that were loaded like hers—with people and blanket-bundles. They passed empty wagons going in the opposite direction. In a few more minutes, they arrived at the train station.

Father stepped down from the front seat of the wagon and reached up a hand to help Kristina jump down, and then turned to help Pani Gregorova. The wooden platform of the station was crowded with more people and more bundles. Whimpering toddlers held their mothers' long skirts, families clung to each other in farewell embraces. Tears. . . everywhere, eyes were filled with tears. It was as though death itself were separating them.

It was time to say goodbye to Father. Kristina wondered if he would cry like the other parents who were saying goodbye to their children. Father had not hugged her or any of her sisters for as long as she could remember, maybe not ever. Embarrassed, she put her arms around his tall, bony frame. She had thought she would not be sorry to leave his demanding strictness and cold gruff manners, but suddenly she realized how strong he was and how frail she felt without his strength to protect her. She hugged him tightly and sobbed, unable to let go. Father pressed her head hard into his shoulder.

"Will you come to America some day?"

She had heard her mother ask this question many times. The answer was always the same: "Never." His eyes would cloud up and he'd stare off into space. Mother explained to the girls that when Father was three years old, he had been in a ferryboat that had capsized in the Danube River. His mother and brothers had drowned; he had been rescued, but only after nearly drowning himself. He grew up in an orphanage, and never got over his deathly fear of boats. "When they build a bridge over the Atlantic Ocean, I will come," he said.

Then would this be the last time she ever saw her father? Kristina wondered.

The ground began to tremble.

"Train!" A young boy who had posted himself at the bend in the track ran toward the platform. "Train is coming round the valley!"

The chuff-chuffing of the train soon competed with the sound of wailing and grief, each getting louder with the approach of the still-unseen monster that would steal husband from wife, mother from child, Kristina from Father. Father took out a handkerchief and blew his nose. His eyes were wet.

"Father, I'm afraid!"

"God will protect you, Kristina."

The words did not comfort her. She had stopped hoping for God's protection ever since little Milka had died. And if Father were so sure that God would protect her, why was he so afraid to take the trip to America?

The train cleared the bend, the chuffing stopped as the huge iron monster approached, and the brakes now screeched. Kristina stepped way back from the tracks, pulling Father with her, fearful that the steam spitting engine would either explode or reach out hidden arms and grab her. The monster slowly came to a stop and emitted an enormous sigh. Steam jetted and hissed from under the belly of the gigantic boiler.

A conductor came out of the passenger car and placed a little wooden stool for people to step on to help them get into the train. Pani Gregorova gently put her arm around Kristina's waist.

"Come," she said. "We'll have our lunch on the train."

Kristina let go of her father. With Pani Gregorova's goodness, and anticipating the goodness of the salami, she broke her connection with home. Mother was at the other end of the journey, nine days away.

The inside of the train looked like a long narrow church with its rows of wooden seats. Kristina found an empty seat next to a window, tucked her large bundle under the seat, and waved, waiting for Father's searching glance to find her. The whistle blew one long blast, the engine began to chuff, and the train creaked and lurched and agonized its way out of the station. She waved to Father, pressing his face permanently in her memory. His eyes had been wet. *He would miss her. He did love her.* This sight of him would have to last the rest of her life.

She placed the fairy tale book on her lap for support, and gingerly unwrapped the package containing her provisions. She took five thick slices of the aromatic salami, and rewrapped the package. From the loaf of rye bread, she tore an enormous chunk, and lay out the largest of the pickles. For once she could have her fill, even though it wasn't Christmas.

Pani Gregorova raised one eyebrow in disapproval of such extravagance, but she did not say a word. Kristina concentrated her full attention, first on inhaling the delicious smells, then on chewing each mouthful slowly, alternating salami, bread, and pickle. After a long while, she smiled. She had eaten enough for her stomach, rather than her father, to say, "no more." And now she was on her way to an unbelievable place where she and her stomach would have that wonderful feeling every day.

Content, she pressed her face up to the glass and watched the countryside go by. It was exciting to see nearby things move by so quickly while the distant hills mysteriously stayed in one place. The train stopped from time to time, and at each stop more travelers got on, but almost no one got off. Soon the car was full, and passengers struggling with bundles crowded the aisles. Finally, the train made no more stops, and left the rolling farmlands.

It labored strenuously up hills, wound around bends, and roared through dark and dreadful tunnels.

It was dark when they arrived in Vienna where they had to change trains. The station in Vienna must be the biggest building in the world, thought Kristina. Marble walls led up to a ceiling higher than any tree she had ever seen. People swarmed in dizzying numbers, speaking in Slovak, Hungarian, German, and other, unfamilar languages. Hundreds of people were waiting with their bundles for the train that would take them to the great ship that would cross the ocean with them to America.

On the next train, seats were padded and windows were cleaner. Kristina leaned into the warm comfort of Pani Gregorova, and quickly fell asleep.

Somewhere in the middle of the night, talking and movement nearby woke her. "It's a border check," explained Pani Gregorova. "Take out your purse with your papers."

Kristina had not heard good things about Germans. Sometimes they took away people's books for no reason. She took out her traveling documents and watched the uniformed inspector stamp them and punch her train ticket. He motioned her to open her bundle, and he poked around in it. *Would he forbid her fairy tale book?* Then he motioned for her to stand while he checked her seat.

"Das is gut," he said. He stamped her

documents and returned them to her and went on to the next passenger.

They had left the great Austro-Hungarian Empire. They were now in Germany.

Kristina pulled aside the little brown curtains on the windows, and pressed her face right up to the window, shading her eyes from the return glare. Total blackness. The meager light from the kerosene lanterns inside the train illuminated the swiftly passing ground for a few feet only.

"So this is Germany," she said to herself.

"What can you see?" asked Pani Gregorova.

"Nothing, only forest." Kristina peered into the depths, looking for wolves, bears, witches and dragons. Those dark, impenetrable woods could be home to any dangerous beings, real or imaginary, she thought. She ate again, but sparingly this time. Two more slices of salami, and it was half gone.

In the morning, the cheery sunlit landscape reinforced her fairy tale ideas of Germany from the night before. The train ran beside a mighty river, and Kristina was thrilled to see one after another magnificent castle commanding a hill in each town on the other side. *Did handsome princes live there? Or wicked Queens?* It was easy to imagine a princess being locked up in one of the towers unable to escape with those massive walls and miniature windows.

Other people in the train stirred now, eating their breakfast, walking up the aisle to the water closet. Children scouted out other children to make friends and propose games. Soon the adults followed to befriend the parents of their children's new acquaintances, and so a social group was formed out of their common destination. Their origins—their various districts of Moravia, Bohemia, and Slovakia, which at first had made them sound strange to each other, now drew them together. After all, their dialects were close enough that they could understand each other, whereas only a few could understand the German conductors. Their common language, common poverty, and common dreams began to bond them into a clan.

"Hamburg! Last stop!" The conductor called out the news first in German, then Hungarian. Excitement filled the train as the passengers rewrapped their bundles, mothers spit-cleaned their children's faces and everyone tried to hand-press the wrinkles out of dresses and suits.

"Oh, will I be glad to move around again," said Pani Gregorova. "My poor bones are aching from sitting so long."

"How will we know how to get to the ship from the train station?" asked Kristina.

"Don't worry. All of these people cannot get lost. A guide will come from the steamship company."

The passengers got down from the train and boarded waiting wagons that carried them to the customs clearinghouse near the docks.

"Look! Is that it? Kristina asked, pointing to a huge black and white ship. "Is that the great *Kaiser Wilhelm der Grosse*? asked Kristina.

"I believe so," said Pani Gregorova, shielding her eyes from the sun for a better look. "It's magnificent, isn't it?"

The massive ship shone in the sunlit afternoon. Four enormous smokestacks rose from its deck. Kristina thought of her mother, and was reassured by the fact that her mother had been on this very ship. It was the newest, fastest steamship in the world. For a second her father's fear of boats flashed in her mind, but this ship was no small ferry. *There was no way for a big ship like this to overturn. . . was there?*

Chapter 3: *The Kaiser Wilhelm der Grosse*

At the emigrant hall, everything seemed in total confusion. Officials in white uniforms were shouting commands in German, but the people did not know where they were supposed to go. With waving arms and whistles, the officials finally separated the men from the women and drove them into separate inspection chambers.

"Quick! Quick! Quick!" was all Kristina could understand. She and Pani Gregorova, along with all the other women and small children from the train, were herded into a large, tile-walled room. Female attendants shouted and gestured with their hands that they were to take off their clothes. Kristina flushed with shame when she understood that she must remove everything.

"Why?" she asked.

The insistent commands of "Quick! Quick! Quick!" told her that there was no choice. The room was filled with naked women's bodies. Their clothing was on a long bench with their traveling bags. The matrons herded the women into a second room, and came to each woman with a handful of a vile-smelling, slippery substance, and indicated that she must rub it all over her body. "Quick! Quick!"

Suddenly a shower of warm water and clouds of steam burst down from pipes in the ceiling. Everyone screamed with the shock, but soon the water had washed off the slippery mess, and the matrons were shouting, "Quick! Quick!" for them to get their clothes and dressed again.

"They must think we didn't wash before dressing to go to America," said Kristina.

"It's because some people have lice, perhaps. They don't want others to get it," explained a tall woman.

In the outer room, there was still more confusion. Clerks were asking questions, checking documents and bundles. Mothers were calling for their children. One woman was shrieking that her money had been stolen, and several men shouted that they had been given the wrong change at the food concession. Shouts in other languages that Kristina could not understand added to the chaos.

At last they were permitted out again into the wide open loading area in front of the great ship. Kristina had not imagined that so many people lived in the entire world as were there moving with her toward the gangplank. There were richly dressed ladies with ruffled skirts, lace blouses and colorful, wide-brimmed hats; elegant men in well-tailored suits, and uniformed servants carrying gleaming wicker luggage. .. .the poor people, with their plainer, rougher clothes and their blanket-wrapped bundles by far outnumbered the rich.

"Will we all fit in that ship?"
asked Kristina in wonder.

A Slovak man near her heard and answered. "The *Kaiser Wilhelm der Grosse* can hold two thousand, three hundred people. All the people of your village, and four others like it could fit in this great ship." Kristina recognized him as a man who had been in the same train with them.

A gate barred the way to Kristina and Pani Gregorova and all the other poor people from the train while the finely-dressed people and their servants carrying their luggage walked up the huge ramp.

"That's first class," explained the Slovak man. "They go to the upper decks, stay in elegant cabins and have many servants to wait on them. We are going to the third class deck, and sleep in the steerage. Ha! You'll see that it's not so fine. But the rich pay sixty-five dollars, and we pay only forty. That's the difference. But we'll all get to America just the same."

When the first and second class passengers had finished boarding, the gate was opened, and the mass of people destined for the steerage were herded up the ramp. A sudden blast from one of the huge smokestacks almost tumbled Kristina over. The talkative Slovak was behind her and put one hand on her shoulder to steady her.

"Don't be afraid," he said. "It will do that two more times."

She was grateful for the warning, and was ready for the next blasts.

At the top of the ramp, an attendant directed them downstairs to the lower deck. There, the women and girls traveling alone were separated from the men and families. Kristina kept close to Pani Gregorova, so she wouldn't lose her in the pushing and bumping mass. Carefully they made their way down the steep, narrow stairway into the woman's quarters. Complaints rose around them.

"It's so dark!"

"I can't see!"

"Ugh!, What a smell!"

"Please don't push!"

"Keep going."

Kerosene lanterns at the opposite end of the hall barely illuminated the long chamber. Two-tiered bunk beds lined each wall, maybe two hundred beds in all. Little portholes let in almost no light at all, because they were under the level of the water. It was impossible to move between the bunks without excusing oneself, bumping and sliding past others, as they looked for two empty beds.

"We are going to be packed in like animals on the way to market!" said Pani Gregorova as she finally located a place for them. "Put your bundle in this drawer under the bunk," she directed.

"Mother wrote that it would be crowded," said Kristina, "but I didn't know how bad it would be. What is that awful smell?"

"It's disinfectant."

Underneath the mask of the disinfectant, however, another odor hung thickly in the crowded quarters: the sour smell of human sweat, dirt, vomit and sickness.

"Ugh. I can't breathe!" gasped Kristina.

"I hope there was no disease among the passengers on the last voyage," worried Pani Gregorova. "If we get sick, we will not be allowed past the inspection at Castle Garden."

"Let's go up onto the deck to get some fresh air at least.

It was a relief to be back in the open, but the deck was full of people and the large bundles that didn't fit down in the steerage. There was barely room to walk and she had to pardon herself constantly as she wound around people standing, sitting, or leaning on the railings.

Kristina found a place to lean, looked out at the sea they would soon be headed for, then at city of Hamburg, and then turned to watch the people around her. She listened intently, trying to make sense of the babbling of many different languages. She knew and understood Hungarian in addition to Slovak, but there were other languages whose words were similar to her own, but not all.

"What are they speaking?"

"That family is speaking Polish," answered Pani Gregorova pointing to her left. "And those men are speaking Russian. Those languages are like cousins of our Slovak language."

As the sun was setting over the sea, a long blast from the main funnel startled them. Engines began to sound, and the crowd became increasingly excited. Slowly the ship began to inch out of port. People chattered excitedly and waved at the receding land. A tall, thin man pulled out a harmonica and played a traditional Slovak melody, a song that had been forbidden in public by the Hungarian soldiers. Other Slovaks rose and began to sing, expanding their chests in pride and freedom. Kristina joined them. There were tears in their eyes when the song was over.

In another section of the deck, a Russian folk song began. It soon mixed with German, Polish, Yiddish, Slovene, Hungarian and Croatian melodies. It was as if each national group were announcing its presence

on the ship. Although they could not speak each other's language, they shared a common poverty and the common wrenching of separation from family and home and were bound for a common destination.

Soon it was dark. One by one, the little children fell asleep, and their mothers descended with them into the dark, airless sleeping quarters. The cool ocean breezes turned chilly, but Kristina wanted to stay above deck with the singers as long as she could keep her eyes open.

Finally Pani Gregorova urged her downstairs. The smell was worse than before. A long line was waiting to use the toilets.

"Only four toilets for two hundred people!

How can we wait?" asked Kristina.

Many people were not waiting, and relieved themselves in basins or pails and carried them upstairs to throw overboard. There was another long line to use the washroom. Kristina was dismayed. She had always been so clean. "How can I go to bed without washing?" she asked Pani Gregorova.

The space for each toilet was exceedingly narrow. Instead of a seat there was an open trough. It was difficult to use, and was already quite filthy. It smelled as bad as the outhouse back in Myjava.

They entered the sleeping quarters, and the noise that hit them was as if the giant engines of the ship were in the same room with them. The loud, rhythmic staccato din made conversation almost impossible. The floor vibrated with the trembling of the unseen machinery.

"We're over the steering screws," shouted Pani Gregorova. "That's why it's called steerage."

The light from the widely spaced kerosene lanterns gave very little help. It was almost impossible to see. Kristina and her guardian had to count the bunks to be sure they reached the right one.

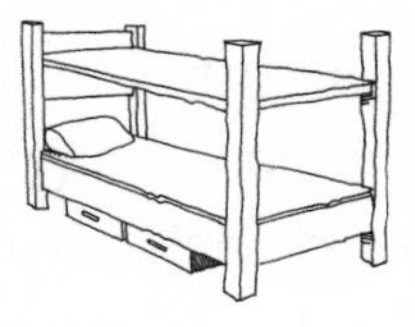

"Is this ours?" Kristina asked.

"Yes, number twenty-three," answered Pani Gregorova. "You'd better remember that."

Kristina carefully slipped out of her dress, took off her high shoes and her black stockings and neatly arranged them in the drawer under the bunk. She took the little pillow from her bundle and placed it at the head of her bed. Pani Gregorova took the upper bunk.

The mattress was thin, not much more than the thickness of a doubled over blanket, and the wood underneath was very hard to Kristina's unpadded bones.

"Good night, Pani Gregorova," she said, as she pulled the little black curtain around her bed. For a few minutes she wondered how she would sleep with the noise of the engines in her ears, but soon her dreams translated the sound into railroad trains and back to the peaceful, natural setting of home and sister, and of gardens, and chickens, and geese.

She stirred. *What was that tickling?* She was too tired to wake completely. She must have imagined it. Sleep claimed her again.

Again in her dreams the tickling. She was now at Farmer Kernak's haymow. Her sister Olga was tickling her leg with a wisp of hay. Kristina brushed the hay away and told her to stop. Now Anna was tickling her back, and Susanna and Betka each had wisps of hay that they drew lightly over her face and stomach. Kristina scratched and rolled over to get away from their teasing. They came at her again.

Suddenly Kristina's eyes snapped open. Her sisters were not there. It was not hay that was tickling her. It was bugs. Bedbugs. Bedbugs were crawling all over her. She bolted upright.

"Youch!" she cracked her head on the wooden bunk overhead. "Pani Gregorova! Pani Gregorova! Wake up! Help me! There are bugs in my mattress.!"

Back at home in Myjava, they had sometimes had an occasional bedbug, but then they would immediately burn their straw mattresses and make new ones. Everything at home was kept spotless and clean. Now there were bugs all over her.

"They are in my mattress, too," said Pani Gregorova. Indeed, all around them, women were complaining and children were whimpering.

"What can we do?" Kristina asked.

"Just kill them." Pani Gregorova picked the bugs one by one off her body, squeezed them and dropped them on the floor. Kristina began to do the same. She swept her mattress with her hand and crawled reluctantly back onto it. She could hear everyone in the steerage compartment slapping and scratching.

She slapped and scratched and squeezed bugs for a long time before exhaustion finally won out and she fell asleep, bugs and all.

Chapter 4: Crossing the Atlantic

Pani Gregorova shook Kristina gently. "Wake up, or you'll miss breakfast."

Kristina opened her eyes. Her first sensation was hunger. Next was the sensation of stiffness and aching in her back and neck and shoulders from the hardness of the bunk. Her head had a large lump from the whack she had gotten; her skin was lumpy and itchy from bug bites. Yet it was, as usual, her empty stomach that got her going each day. She pulled on her stockings, slipped her dress over her head, and buttoned up her shoes.

Everyone in the long line in the corridor outside the ship's galley looked equally aching and weary. Men were unshaven, women's hair uncombed, clothes were wrinkled. They were each holding a tin bowl and cup and a tin spoon. Kristina saw a huge pile of dented utensils in a large open bin; she selected a bowl and a cup and joined the end of the line. Every one in line was scratching.

The line slowly advanced, and in the next

corridor she could see a sailor at the other end ladling out a gray, soupy mixture. She sniffed. It was not a familiar smell. When it was her turn, she held out her bowl and the steward slopped a large ladle-full into it, splashing the sides so there was no clean space for her fingers to hold it.

"What is it?" she asked, in Slovak; then when he didn't respond, she asked again in Hungarian.

The steward looked at her blankly and growled something in German. Another steward filled her cup with coffee and indicated to her with an impatient jerk of his head that she was not to dawdle in line, but move on quickly. There was a tray with slices of bread, and she gladly took one.

She carried her cup and bowl through a wide doorway that led to a huge, noisy dining room, already holding hundreds of steerage passengers. She found an unoccupied bare wooden table and sat on the backless bench. She stirred the gruel around with her tin spoon, then cut into the unrecognizable lumps to discover what they were. Some were potato, some were tough masses of dough. The unappetizing smell made her hesitate. She was hungry, but was this safe to eat?

Below, in the sleeping quarters, in the drawer under her bunk, she still had enough salami for one satisfying meal. Or two light meals. Or four snacks to go along with something else edible. Now that the salami was so close to being gone, she had decided to make the remainder last as long as possible so she could savor the thought during the day that it would be there, to comfort her with its smell, its tasty chewiness in the evening. But if she couldn't eat this gruel she had been given, she would have to eat her salami for breakfast, and it would be quickly gone.

She gingerly put the spoon in and said a small prayer as she opened her mouth and closed her nose. It was all she could do to swallow. She quickly bit into the bread to dull the taste in her mouth.

Pani Gregorova arrived at the table with her own bowl of gruel. She sat down on the bench opposite Kristina. "The line is so long. We must get up earlier tomorrow. I am starving. Is it any good?" she asked.

"No, it's dreadful."

Kristina watched as Pani Gregorova sniffed the bowl up close. She knew that Pani Gregorova's supply of extra provisions was gone because she had shared them with another family on the train. Kristina hoped that her guardian would be able to stomach the gruel. It would be difficult to have to share any part of her salami. She held her nose and quickly scooped up spoonful after spoonful of the stuff and with large deliberate swallows was able to empty her plate and fill her stomach.

She was relieved to see that Pani Gregorova also ate it without complaining.

They brought their utensils back to the galley, and learned that they must wash them themselves, down in the washroom. No soap was given, and the sea water from the tap was cold. They were to keep the same plate and cup for the rest of the trip.

After storing the utensils at their bunk, Kristina and Pani Gregorova went up on the deck. People lined the railings on either side, watching the sea. A large group was seated around one man; animated conversation and laughter emanated from the group. Kristina saw that the center of their attention was the talkative Slovak she had met yesterday. She found an empty place on a bench and listened.

"Pan Martin, are the buildings in New York really as tall as thirty houses?

"Pan Martin, how much can a man make in a shoe factory?"

"Pan Martin, do you speak English?"

"Is it hard to learn?

"Tell us about the Statue of Liberty."

"How far is Chicago?"

"Do you know my cousin Jan Dvorsky in Lansford, Pennsylvania?"

The questions were endless, and the good-natured Pan Martin answered and joked and entertained them with stories filled with strange words for things they had never seen in the small towns of Slovakia. *Trolley, elevated, automobile, banana*. Places unheard of—*Manhattan, Hudson, Guttenberg, Uptown*. Streets in the magic city of New York had numbers for names, numbers like *Second Avenue, Eighty-sixth Street*. How huge the city must be! Streets hadn't needed names or numbers in Myjava. There was only one street through the center of town, and any road that led to a farm or orchard or woodlot was just called "Michek's road" or "the road to Klc's woodlot."

"I've been on this ship many times," Pan Martin told them. He had begun a business in America, selling belts that he made in his own little shop. One by one, he had brought four children over to the New Country, and now he was bringing his wife and his youngest child. Kristina liked being near him. He looked a bit like Father, with his dark wavy hair, large nose and big silky mustache, but he was taller, and strong, and well-fed. And Father had never been so jolly and full of warm good humor.

A loud bell signaled lunchtime. When she got to the galley line, Kristina was disappointed to smell the same gruel as the morning's breakfast. Others were upset too. Everyone grumbled, and a few men dared to ask, "Isn't there something else? This food isn't fit for animals!" The stewards shrugged their shoulders and muttered in German.

If the grown men didn't like it either, and there was nothing *they* could do about it, thought Kristina, then she would have to be satisfied with lumpy gray gruel or nothing . . . Unless she tapped the secret salami hidden under her bunk!

She left the line and went to the entrance to the steerage quarters. She had been breathing fresh ocean breezes for the past half hour and as she descended the stairs, the heavy, stinking air in the sleeping quarters was worse than she remembered. She stepped backwards up the stairs, took a deep breath of cleaner air, filled her lungs, and hoped she could get to her bunk and back without breathing.

In the semi-darkness, she counted bunks to

find hers. Nervously, she looked around to see if anyone was watching, and pulled the little bundle out from under the bed. She carefully untied the napkin and lovingly positioned the salami on the lower bunk to cut it. She pulled back her hand in horror. Breathing in the foul air, it was no longer a focus of her concerns. Her salami, her beautiful, life-saving salami was covered with bugs. Evil, crawling little bugs, waving their antenna in the dim light. Hundreds of them were tunneling through her precious treasure. She screamed in rage.

"What's the matter?" A few women who had been below came over to her side.

"Ahgh!" Kristina gestured at the bundle. She could not speak. Tears filled her eyes.

"You'd better throw it away," one woman advised. "Those bugs are probably filled with disease."

"That's a shame," said the other. "You should keep your food in a tin container next time. With a tight lid."

Kristina wrapped the salami back in its napkin. She carried it by one corner, holding it as far away from her body as she could manage, and went up the narrow stairs to the deck. She clenched her teeth, opened the napkin and heaved her treasure over the railing. With a little "Kachunk!," it disappeared into the quickly passing waters.

Soberly, she got into the galley line, accepted the lumpy gruel, and ate it.

Supper, incredibly, was exactly the same. There was even more grumbling, with no results. But by the late evening, not many of the passengers worried whether the gruel would be offered again for breakfast. The gentle ocean breeze had become a determined wind and the great *Kaiser Wilhelm der Grosse* rocked from side to side in the rolling waves.

There was no place to throw up except over the railing. Many passengers did not reach the railing in time. They vomited on the floors, on the benches, in their beds. A German porter worked all evening mopping the decks.

"Katsen? Katsen?" he said cheerfully as he

sloshed the mop around. *"Are you vomiting again?"* He sloshed and spread and thinned the vomit into a sticky film coating the entire deck. The smell made the people even sicker.

The gruel tasted only slightly worse coming up than it had going down. Kristina was surprised at the number of times she heaved. How could there be anything left in her stomach? The disturbing, upset feeling continued even after she had totally emptied her insides over the railing. Despite the now even more sickly air in the steerage below, she went down to her bunk to shiver with weakness and misery.

That evening, that night, and another whole day Kristina and many of the other passengers spent entirely in bed. If they had anything left to vomit, their small tin plates served to catch it. A few women who were not ill borrowed buckets from the sailors and made the rounds of the bunks to empty the plates and then carried the buckets to dump over the railing.

Finally the wind calmed, and the ship stopped rolling. The stomachs stopped rolling as well. Life felt good again to Kristina as she climbed up the stairs into the fresh air and the morning sunshine of the third day at sea. It was good to stand by the railing and watch for flying fish or whale spouts. Sometimes they saw a ship going in the opposite direction, back to Europe. In the afternoon, the small children napped, the men set up card games and the women sewed or crocheted. Here and there an argument developed because of the lack of seating space, or the racing around of the smaller children. Kristina found a corner and kept to it, reading her book of wonderful tales of princesses and kings, of monsters and fairies. Although she had read it many times before, the stories were richer and had new meaning with each new reading. A scene of one of the stories was in the grand dining room of a palace, which reminded her of what Pan Martin had said about the first class decks. She burned with curiosity to see how the rich people traveled.

"Let's go up and look around the upper decks," she said to Pani Gregorova.

"We aren't allowed up."

"Why not? The first class passengers come down here to walk about and gape at us." At that moment there were several fine ladies with bustled dresses, beautifully coiffured hair, and lacy blouses strolling around like tourists, offering candy to the children.

"They say we smell bad," said Pani Gregorova.

"Of course we smell bad. There's no decent place to wash, and there are too many of us packed into such crowded quarters."

"Well, the first class passengers pay to have the run of the ship, and we pay only for steerage."

"I would just love to have one

look." said Kristina wistfully.

"*Hsst*. Follow me," said a tall, elegant gentlewoman who had stood behind Kristina, overhearing her. "If they stop you, I will say I have hired you as my maidservant. But promise, take one quick look, and then you must return."

"Oh, thank you, thank you, thank you, kind lady!" Kristina felt as though she had been touched by a real live fairy godmother. That feeling was greatly magnified when she reached the top of the sets of stairs that led to the upper deck. Having gotten Kristina past the sailor who stood guard at the connecting stairway, the lady waved goodbye and went to join her friends.

Kristina stood alone in the vast dining room. It was far, far better than the fairy tale. Large tables covered with fine white linen cloths were set with elegant china plates and gleaming silver. The chairs all had velvet upholstery and lace doilies on the backs. Two sides of the dining room were paneled with mirrors with elegant carved oak woodwork in between. Long panels of paintings of serene landscapes and sunny skies lined the third wall. Crystal chandeliers sparkled like thousands of diamonds. Kristina had never in her life imagined anything so breathtakingly beautiful. Stewards in white uniforms came in through the swinging doors carrying baskets of bread and dishes of fancy vegetables and pickles. They placed a basket and a

dish on each table. Others brought silver pitchers from which they poured water into sparkling glasses.

Kristina envied the stewards. What a marvelous place to work! One of them looked up at her and said something to her in German. Kristina, frightened at being discovered where she didn't belong, quickly retreated, scampering down the stairway to the crowded third class deck.

Pani Gregorova marveled at the descriptions of the dining room as she and Kristina both stoically choked down the gruel from their dripping tin plates. After that, the sights and smells of the steerage were even more distasteful to Kristina. Everything was sticky to the touch, disgusting to the smell. The crowd and the noise of the arguing, pushing people, crying babies, and the babble of languages irritated every sense. She strove to maintain some of the peace and refinement in her spirit from the dining room upstairs.

"After dinner I must go for lessons," Pani Gregorova said.

"Where? What kind of lessons?" asked Kristina.

"Pan Martin has offered to teach us how to answer the questions the clerks will ask us at Castle Garden. People can get confused when they enter America, because of the language."

"Castle Garden! It sounds like a wonderful place! Is it really a castle? With beautiful flowers?"

"No, not at all," said Pan Martin, who was passing by as they ate. "Many years ago, immigrants were inspected at a fort called Castle Garden, in New York. But so many people started to come to America, the Castle Garden inspection station wasn't big enough. So the government made a new place; it's on Ellis Island. But everyone who had gone through

Castle Garden wrote home about it, and for years the next family members who came thought the place they were inspected was Castle Garden. Since they didn't speak English, it never was corrected."

"What questions will the inspectors ask me?"

"You will not have to answer. You are under fifteen." said Pani Gregorova. "I'll answer for you. You have only to pass the medical inspection."

"But we had a medical inspection at Hamburg."

"They are much stricter in America," said Pani Gregorova. "And if someone fails, they will send that person back to Hamburg on this ship."

"What if a wife passes inspection, but her husband fails?"

"The ship must carry the husband back to Hamburg free of charge, but if the wife wants to go back with him, she has to pay the fare."

"But if one child fails, what does the rest of the family do?"

"If a child fails, the ship will take the mother back as well."

"And if there are many children, and only one fails? What is the mother to do?"

"I don't know Kristina. I don't know."

"And how would someone get back to

Slovakia, or Moravia, or Hungary? Does the ship pay for the train back to their home?"

"No, only to Hamburg."

Kristina imagined herself being sent back, stranded in Hamburg with no money to reach home. She was glad she would not have to answer any questions. When she was frightened, she forgot even the simplest things.

"Pan Martin, do you think some of the people on this ship will be sent back to Hamburg?" asked Kristina.

Pan Martin's face became very serious. "I have been through four inspections. Of the two thousand people, about forty or so are sure to fail the inspection."

"Oh, how miserable that must be. Now I understand why Mother said Castle Garden is called *the Island of Tears.*"

On the sixth day of the voyage, the passengers were suddenly awakened by being nearly tossed out of their beds, and the sounds of objects hitting the floor. Whatever wasn't fastened down was rolling and sliding as the floor underneath them heaved first up to one side and then to the other. Tin plates rattled and clanged, babies fell out of bunks, and screamed.

Kristina located Pani Gregorova in the darkness. "What's happening?" she screamed.

"I don't know," shouted Pani Gregorova. "I think it's a storm." Others were crowding and pushing to get out onto the deck. Kristina and Pani Gregorova, clinging carefully to the guardrail, followed the others. It was almost impossible to walk as the sense of up, down, and sideways was in total confusion from the great heaving motion of the ship.

On the deck, the clouds were low and dark and moving fast. The wind was horrible. The noise of loose metal banging against the sides of the ship added to the dreadful howling of the gale. Kristina's loosely tied kerchief was snatched from her neck, and before she could grab it, was sucked up out of reach, flying like a crippled bird with one wing. Other objects were flying off the ship too, hats, glasses, even the deck hand's mop. Children were screaming in panic. The sailors were shouting orders in German.

"Get below! Get below!" But it was impossible. More people were coming out on the deck.

"If we're going to die, let us die. What good will it do to get below?" asked a woman with a small child in her arms.

The sight of the sea, with waves as high as the ship was terrifying. One wave hit the ship broadside. The deck tilted up with such suddenness and angle that everyone was thrown shrieking to the opposite railing. Pan Martin was among them. He grabbed hold of the railing and began to yell. *"Zbohom, zena moha! Zbohom, deti moje*! Goodbye my good wife! Goodbye my children! This is the end of us. Good bye! Good bye!"

Kristina held on to Pani Gregorova and screamed. If Pan Martin who knew everything, who had been on this very ship so many times knew that the ship was sinking, then there was no hope. It was really the end. Father's fears had come true.

"I don't want to die!" she screamed. "Pani Gregorova, why must we all die!"

Her guardian did not answer. She held on to Kristina as tightly as Kristina held her.

"I want to see my mother before I die!"

The wind and high seas raged on throughout the afternoon. As the day's darkness turned to night's pitch blackness, a fierce, hammering rain began. Bullets of rain smashed into their faces and quickly soaked their clothing. Slowly the masses of people groped their way back to their bunks.

Exhausted, drenched, nauseated, and totally despairing, Kristina lay in her bed sobbing, and for once not challenging the rights of the bedbugs to crawl on her. *As I crushed the life out of you, little bugs, so God is crushing the life out of us. We are nothing more to God than bedbugs,* she thought. *If only I could have seen my mother before I died.*

Chapter 5: Ellis Island

When she awoke, the room was level. Women were dressing, talking excitedly. The sun was cheerfully flashing in the water outside the portholes. "Look! Come, look! Come on deck! It's the Statue of Liberty!"

"Are we dead? Is the Statue of Liberty in Heaven?"

"No, we are alive!" said Pani Gregorova. "The storm is over. It's better than Heaven. We have arrived in America."

Kristina scrambled up the stairs to see for herself. There was land all around them. Land—with buildings—a strange sight for eyes that had seen nothing on the horizon for days except sea. Now, tall buildings were almost close enough to touch.

Everyone was pointing. Kristina turned to see. A soft, little "Oh" escaped her lips. She filled her lungs with the fresh sea air and stood perfectly still. It was larger and more beautiful than she had ever imagined!

So this is the Statue of Liberty! And this is America . . the land that would be her home. Here is where she would work, and have money and enough to eat. Here is where her mother lived! She had thought her eyes had used up all

their tears during the storm, but they filled once more.

All around her, people were laughing and hugging each other, pinching themselves, kissing their children. A few got on their hands and knees, and then the rest followed, to give thanks to God for delivering them through the storm into the sight of the marvelous Statue of Liberty, the Beautiful Lady of their dreams. Kristina remembered her last thoughts of the night before. She knelt with the others and wept with joy.

Pani Gregorova put her arm around Kristina's waist. "You're all damp. Come change your clothes and get ready to see your mother."

Kristina was dressed and had her bundles

repacked long before the huge ship nestled into its dock. The steerage passengers watched, fascinated, as little tugboats manipulated the big carcass of the *Kaiser Wilhelm* into its parking place. At last the gangways opened up. "Look, the first and second class passengers are getting off now. Will they go to Ellis Island first?" Kristina asked.

"No. They won't go to Ellis Island at all," answered Pan Martin.

"Why not?"

"They have already passed inspection."

"How could they do that?"

"An inspector and a doctor come on board up there and check them out. They paid a higher fare, so the government knows that they will not become charity cases. They are not asked so many questions or checked for diseases. It's over very quickly and they can go on their way."

Solid, unmoving land was a strange sensation under her feet as she stepped off the ramp onto the firm ground of New Jersey. Her legs had become so used to the instabilities of the ship that now muscles reacted with disbelief at having no need to exert any balancing efforts.

"Land! Land! Solid land!" people were

shouting all around her. Some got down and kissed the grass and soil.

"America! America! America!" One couple was dancing around and around but their land legs had not come back, and they fell laughing in a heap.

The joy and excitement all around her matched Kristina's own. But she would not kiss the ground. It wasn't land that would mark her arrival, it was her mother. And she wanted her lips to be clean!

The mass of steerage passengers were herded slowly past customs officers who checked their baggage. Then they were herded to another dock where they boarded big open barges for a short ride to a low flat island. Ellis Island. The mass of people swarmed off the barge, then headed across the open space to the huge ornate building in front of them.

Inside, Kristina felt blinded until her eyes adjusted to being out of the sun. The ceiling was so high over her head she could not see the details of it. Gatemen hurried them on, directed them to lines for inspection. The building was filled with a loud hum from the sound of hundreds of people speaking in a multitude of languages. People were carrying and pushing along huge bundles, trunks, and suitcases of every description. They were hastened up a huge staircase.

Kristina heard whisperings that there were

doctors at the head of the stairs who watched how you walked. They wouldn't let lame people into the country. If someone huffed and puffed after climbing the stairs, the doctors would think the person had heart disease. Kristina watched as an old man with a limp hobbled up the stairs in front of her. He had tried to hide it when they were on the first floor, by pretending to push his bundle along with his stiff leg, but that was impossible to do on the stairs. The doctor had stopped him, wrote the letter L on his

coat collar and sent him to an enclosed cage where others were waiting with letters on their collars. *What did those letters mean? Were these people going to have to return to Hamburg?* Kristina shivered.

Kristina was gestured to get into a line to be inspected. Pani Gregorova was directed to another line. When Kristina's turn came, an attendant signaled her to take off her upper garments. The doctor in white uniform put his stethoscope to her chest, and she flushed with embarrassment. He said a few words and she understood that she must open her mouth wide for him to press down her tongue and check her throat. He looked at her skin. Kristina tried hard not to scratch the bites on her arms, chest and legs. But there was now a new itch in her scalp that was becoming unbearable. The doctor looked a moment at the bites, but said nothing. She passed on to a new line.

It was this second inspection that she most feared. *Was her mother on the other side of the building?* Kristina could see a waiting crowd on the other side of a huge iron gate. Mother had written that she would be there. *What if she weren't! What if she couldn't wait so long and had to go back to her job!* Kristina ached to see her and this last obstacle seemed the longest and cruelest.

As the immigrants walked to the doctor, he stood directly in the path, holding an instrument that looked like a button hook in his hand.

Kristina watched as each immigrant in the line in front of her stopped short and lifted his head to face the doctor. He reached quickly, caught the person's eyelid with his thumb and finger, and turned it back with the button hook to peer under the lid. It was going to hurt. Children who had just undergone this inspection were screaming with pain. Nurses waited with towels and basins.

Finally it was her turn to be checked. *Ahhhhggg.* It was a horrible sensation. It felt as though her eyelid was being ripped. The doctor made a sour face and shook his head. *What was wrong?* He took up a large piece of white chalk, and wrote the letter C+ on a slip of paper which he pinned to the shoulder of Kristina's brown dress.

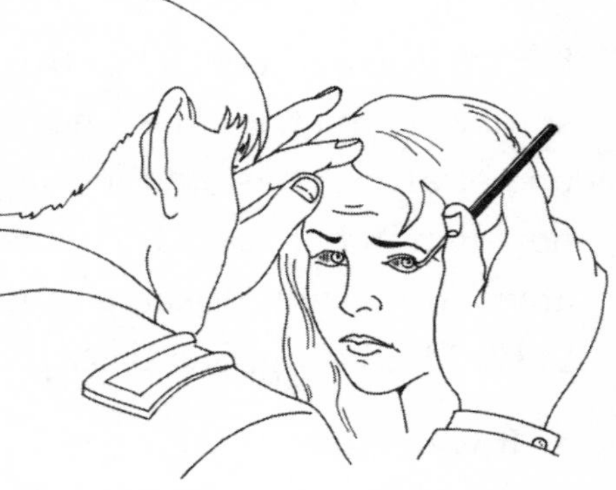

"Why? What's wrong?" Panic rose from deep within her.

The doctor did not speak Slovak. An attendant took her arm and led her to the caged waiting pen. *This was the place where they gathered the people who were to be sent back to Europe!* Pani Gregorova was watching Kristina from a different line great distance away. There was horror on her face.

"What's wrong with me?" cried Kristina.

"Do you speak Hungarian?" the attendant asked.

"Yes," she said, glad someone could explain.

"It's your eyes. It seems you might have trachoma. It's an eye disease. Many have it. It causes blindness, so no one who has the disease may enter into America. You will be checked by another doctor."

Not enter America! To have lived through the storm and not get through, not see her mother! The agony of the thought made her feel faint. She numbly took a seat on the bench. "My mother. My mother. I want to see my mother," she sobbed.

A tall, older woman in brown wraps was already seated on the bench. She was also weeping. Kristina recognized her from the boat. The woman looked up. "Why have you been put into this area?" she asked.

"They say I have an infection in my eyes. I don't. I can see very well. A doctor checked me in Myjava. I got so many inoculations."

"Your eyes do look very sore," the woman said. She took out a tiny speckled mirror from the bundle at her feet, and held it up for Kristina to see. Kristina looked into the mirror and could not believe it was her own face she saw. Her eyes were red and glassy; the lids were swollen and shiny, and dark circles under her eyes looked as though they had been painted on. *This was not the face she had left her father's house with!*

Could she have caught trachoma along with all the other itches and ailments of the steerage? Would she really go blind? Blind? No, it couldn't be!

"Maybe it's because I was crying all night. I thought the ship was going to sink. I thought we were going to drown." *Would it have been better to drown than be sent back to Hamburg without seeing her Mother?*

When at last it was Kristina's turn to be checked by the supervising doctor, the woman stayed with her to explain in German. "She has been crying, that's all. She has no infection," she said.

The doctor looked carefully at Kristina to determine if this were true. Kristina did not know what was being said, and she began to cry again. The doctor patted her on the head and gently pinched her cheek. He nodded and said something in German.

Her acquaintance translated for her to Hungarian. "It's OK. You pass." With these magic words, Kristina breathed again. She waited a few moments to see how her acquaintance fared with the doctor. She also passed, and redeemed from the humiliation, and the total horror of returning to Europe. She hugged Kristina in her joy.

"We are saved!" she said.

"I will never forget this moment for as long as I live!" said Kristina. "It was the most horrible, and it has changed into the most wonderful!"

A few moments later she was allowed to walk down the exit stairs. She heard her name announced and she was free to enter America. She walked through the huge gates that the other Slovaks had called the Gateway to Paradise. Outside, hundreds of faces were turned towards her—*which one was her mother's?*

Oh! There was Pani Gregorova. She had gotten through inspection much more quickly. A tall man was with her. *That must be her husband*. Kristina had not seen Pan Gregor for three years. How different he looked in American clothes. He had shaved off his mustache, and he seemed taller and stronger. On the other side of Pani Gregorova was a large strong woman in a highly ruffled, long, dark blue dress.

On her head was a straw hat with so many flowers on it, It looked like a garden. Kristina ran to her, dropped her bundle and threw her arms around this beautiful woman. But the woman pulled back and stared hard at Kristina's face. She looked surprised and bewildered.

Could it be that her own mother didn't recognize her?

"Mother!"

"Is that you, Kristina?"

"Mother, yes, it's me! Don't you know me?"

"My Kristina? Your eyes!"

"It's nothing. I was crying."

"And you're so small. I thought you would be much bigger. Didn't you eat anything in these two years?"

Mother started to cry and she grabbed Kristina close to her, holding her tight with warm, strong arms. "I missed you so much! My darling Kristina!" She kissed her cheeks and her forehead and squeezed her again and again. They did not let go of each other for a long, long time. Then they kissed and hugged and laughed and hugged and laughed again. Mother took out one handkerchief for herself and a second one for Kristina and they blew their noses and dried their eyes.

"Am I dreaming? Oh, Mother, am I with

you at last?" The years of aching, of wanting to be held by her mother were all behind her now. She would be in the same city with her mother, and for this moment, she could hold her as hard and as long as she liked. She soaked in her mother's warmth and strength as a desert traveler would drink water after a long, dry, lonely journey. There was no need to talk, no need for anything but the wonderful warmth of her mother's presence.

At last Kristina had enough of holding to be able to stand back and look at this woman. . . . so strong, so beautiful, so elegant in American clothes.

"You must be very tired," said mother. "And I know you will want some home-cooked Slovak food after the ship's food." *Mother was so right.*

After a few minutes conversation of goodbyes and thank-yous, Kristina and her mother said goodbye to the Gregors who were taking a barge to New Jersey where they would take a train to Pennsylvania. Kristina would be going in the opposite direction, on a large ferry to Manhattan.

"And as we travel, you must tell me all about your trip. And how is father? And how are Betka, and Anna, Olga and Susanna?" Mother picked up Kristina's bundle, and they boarded the barge that would take them to Manhattan.

Chapter 6: New York City

None of Mother's letters or Pan Martin's stories on the ship had prepared Kristina for the sights she saw. Buildings stuck like stone spikes up towards the sky. Glass windows reflected the pink western sky of the late afternoon. Kristina counted the windows. *Thirty stories tall! However did people climb all those stairs?*

The narrow streets between the tall buildings were dark canyons, with hordes of well-dressed people walking full speed in both directions. Horses pulling wagons and fancy carriages clattered on the uneven cobbles of the narrow roadway. Kristina and her mother walked to what seemed to be a huge, endless bridge that rose three stories high. A horrible noise thundered overhead and shook the entire structure. Kristina was terrified. A monstrous smoke chuffing train was screeching to a stop. She shrank into the doorway of a store, fearing the entire bridge would

come crashing down on her and her mother.

"Don't worry, It's quite strong," assured

Mother. "It's an elevated train. They call it the 'el'." Come, we're going up those stairs so we can catch the next train uptown."

"Are you sure it's safe?" Kristina did not want to doubt her mother but it looked ominous.

"I ride it often. You will too."

Not if I don't have to, Kristina promised herself as she climbed the stairs leading high above the street.

"You'll soon get used to everything. It takes a while for a greenhorn to adjust to the strange new things in America."

"Greenhorn? What is a greenhorn?"

"You, darling. A greenhorn is a beginner, a new person, like a young cow or goat with soft horns that can't defend itself. You have to be careful because it is very easy for other people to play tricks on a greenhorn, and sometimes cheat them. It's important to learn English as soon as you can."

"Yes. I will learn English as quickly as I can." It was Kristina's second promise to herself.

"It's difficult to be a greenhorn," continued Mother. So many things are new. You'll make a lot of mistakes. It takes a lot of courage to be in a new country."

At a landing there was a little ticket booth. Mother bought two tickets, and gave one to Kristina. The elevated structure began

to rumble and shake. Kristina froze.

"Hurry! The train is coming!" They ran up the next flight of stairs onto the landing. Kristina watched, big-eyed as the train chugged into the station. A uniformed man took the ticket, and mother whisked Kristina into the open door of the train.

There were many empty seats on the woven, straw-covered benches that lined the sides of the car. They sat down, both breathless.

There was so much to look at! Kristina marveled at the clothes people wore, so colorful, so varied. The hats on the women were works of art. Or gardens. Some had bouquets of flowers, others seemed to be baskets of fruit. Women wearing sparkling jewelry and men in well-pressed suits sat riding next to men in poor rags. She didn't understand. Why should there be rags in America?

The view from the window of the train made her eyes open wider and wider. They passed street after street lined with pushcarts filled with goods to sell. She saw tomatoes, heads of lettuce, cucumbers, apples. The colors delighted her, and her mouth dripped, making her swallow. *The stories about America were all true—just look at all the food! Oranges for sale!* She had had oranges only at Christmas. The sight of them brought quick memories of their juicy, tangy-sweetness, and the rich oil in the peel that long ago Mother had taught her to rub on her skin to make it tingle and glow.

Almost every cart she saw had the same thick greenish yellow bunch of spike-like objects. It was very curious. The spikes couldn't be leaves, nor petals. They seemed to be some sort of vegetable.

"What are those, Mother?"

"Those?"

"The greenish-yellow things on the vegetable carts."

Mother looked down out the window, and then smiled. "Those are bananas. They're good to eat."

"Not for me. I'm going to eat oranges."

"You'll see. You'll like bananas, too. And lots of other things you've never eaten before."

"Oh, Mother, I'm so happy to be in America!"

The train rattled on, stopping at station after station. People got on, people got off. Kristina could now see right into the windows of the apartment houses lining the street. She saw women working in their kitchens, children hanging out of windows to watch the train, people sleeping in bed. Clothes hung on hundreds of lines between buildings and on top of buildings. *How did they get the clothes out to the middle of the line when the window was so high up?* There were mysteries

in America. Hanging the wash on the fence seemed easy compared with what women would have to do to get the clothes way out on that rope strung between buildings. She hoped that she would not be asked to do such a dangerous thing on her job.

They arrived at 50th Street and descended

the clanging iron stairs to the street level.

"We'll have to walk a few blocks," Mother said. "Try to remember the neighborhood so you won't get lost when you're by yourself."

The street was filthy, crowded with horses and wagons, horses and carriages, and policemen on horses clopping over the cobbled streets. Trolleys pulled by horses clanged past, then an undertaker's wagon. The people in the streets seemed restless, hurrying in a mad haste to get where they were going. They didn't stop to greet each other as everyone did in Myjava. Gusts of wind blew dirt and papers around. Suddenly a clanging and whistling louder than all the other noises made everyone's head turn. It was a rapid team of horses pulling a fire engine. New York City was noisier even than the steerage.

The fire engine disappeared around a corner and next among the clopping noises of horses and carriage wheels, came a weird chugging and popping sound that could be heard above the general din. A man sat high up on a driver's seat on the front of a strangely-shaped contraption, turning a wheel that poked up on a long pipe from the lower part of the monstrosity. Kristina half expected to see strong men pushing the huge object from behind. There were none.

That must be an auto-mobile. Mother had written about them and Pan Martin had told stories about his ride in one. Kristina stared at it until its chugging, bouncing shape was out of sight among the other traffic. *Things were strange, very strange, here in America.*

Mother guided her across the street.

"Watch your step!"

Staring around at all the sights,

Kristina had almost marched straight
into a pile of horse droppings.

"Whoops!"

"You have to look down when you cross the street, as well as from side to side for the traffic. There is danger from all directions! Even from below."

The horse droppings in the street gave a familiar country smell to the bustling street. But back home in Myjava, such droppings would have been quickly picked up by some farmer to add to his fertilizer pile. Horses and cows were scarce since so many had been slaughtered to eat during the hungry years, and their manure was precious for the gardens and farms. Now she noticed that there were droppings all over the street. Of course, with so many horses around, and all in such a hurry, and no farmers, what would you expect?

As they neared the other side of the street, a new smell caught Kristina's attention: Fresh baked sweet cakes, an aroma warm and yeasty, sweet and heavy in the air. It intoxicated her. She located the bakery a few doors down. There was no need to read the English words on the store in front. In the window were cakes, cookies, pies, rolls, doughnuts, and loaves of shiny-crusted bread dotted with caraway seeds. She stared and inhaled, and was unable to move from all that goodness.

Her mother stopped too, and hugged

her. "Everything's ready at Melceks'. You will have plenty to eat there."

As they climbed the stairs, different cooking smells greeted them on each landing. Kristina stopped, not so much to rest but to enjoy each offering to her nose. The Melceks lived on the fifth floor. "The top floor," said Mother. "It's the best because you can get the most sunshine. The apartments on the lower floors are dark. The windows only face other apartments across the alley."

A crowd of her mother's friends were in the tiny apartment, awaiting Kristina's arrival. A table was spread with a feast: a huge pot of *goulash*—meat and potatoes in a paprika and onion gravy—fruits, cheese, and fancy cakes. And there were those funny yellow bananas. And oranges! It was a party to celebrate her arrival in America. Kristina recognized some of the people as old neighbors from Myjava who had left years ago. She didn't know which way to turn first, but the table with its delights won out.

She clapped her hands in amazement. "Oh, Mother, what a feast!"

Everyone laughed and then they clapped, too.

"My husband works in a bakery, and they let him have the things that are not in perfect shape, or a little burnt at the edges," explained Pani Melcek. "First, wash up. Then come, sit and help yourself. And tell us about your trip and how things are in Myjava."

The bathroom with a sink and running water intrigued her. A large tank over the toillet had a pull chain on it, and water rushed down into the toilet basin and flushed away the contents of the basin, rushing around in circles. She opened and closed the tap in the sink to see water easily pouring out in a rapid stream. There would be no more hauling of buckets in America!

It was heaven to bite into the bread spread with real butter! Everyone pressed her with questions as she ate. She had messages for many of them in her neck purse, which she carefully opened and handed out.

After a marvelous bowl of *goulash,* then cakes and sweet, fresh, cold milk, Kristina looked at the clump of bananas. Pan Melcek was watching her, and broke one off from the bunch.

"Here, eat it."

"No, thank you."

"It's good. Like this, you just peel it. If it's yellow, it's good. If it's green, it's not ripe yet."

The peel he was taking off the banana he offered her was perfectly yellow, with a few thin brown lines on it.

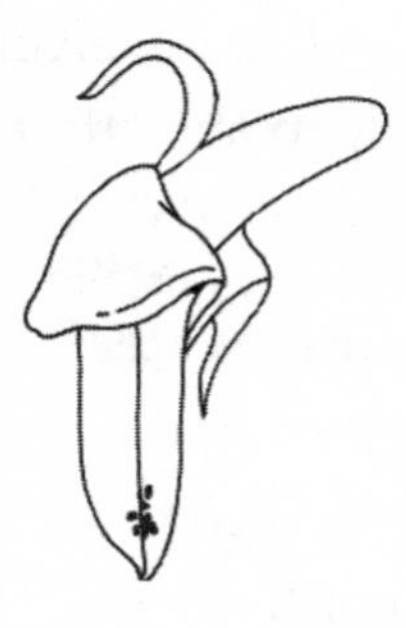

"I don't think I'd like them."

He cut her a slice of the white flesh of the banana, and offered it.

It was strange. Too strange. She was not hungry anymore as she had been on the ship and had forced the German gruel into her empty stomach. She shook her head.

Pan Melcek laughed. "You'll change your mind."

The evening went quickly with Kristina's stories of her trip, conditions back in Myjava, and hearing the myriad of stories and advice everyone was giving her. Finally, they left, and Kristina was exhausted. Now her head itched unmercifully.

"Mother, I'm afraid I have bugs in my hair."

"Ah, ah. That's very possible. I got lice myself from the passage."

"What can I do?"

"We'll fix you up with the kerosene treatment, don't worry."

Mother arranged a basin in the sink, gave Kristina a towel to cover her eyes and nose, and cautioned her not to inhale the poisonous fumes while the kerosene was being poured through her hair. Mother rubbed and worked the kerosene deep into the scalp, while Kristina coughed and choked. The kerosene that

was caught
in the basin
was returned
to a pot
and poured
through her
hair again
and again. It
burned the
scratches like
hot knives,
cutting
through
her scalp.

"Now you leave it on for a half hour more. After that, they'll all be dead. We can comb out the eggs. Then a good hot bath."

A soap shampoo followed, and at last the burning stopped. The smell became tolerable, and it was a great relief to be clean, to be on dry land, to be itch-free, to have a full belly, and best of all, to be on the same side of the ocean as Mother.

But all too soon, Mother kissed her good night, and said, "I have to go now. My employers want me to cook them an early breakfast, so I must be at work.

"Where is your job?" asked Kristina.

"Not so far from here," said Mother. On Seventy-eighth street. Just two stops on the elevated train."

Kristina sighed. It was so close, and still so far. She wanted to hold her mother near her forever. "I will see you tomorrow, at two. I have a break for a few hours. I will take you to your new job."

The Melcek's home was a way-station for new arrivals from Myjava. Their own modest success in the bakery business, and not having children of their own enabled them to have a little room to spare. It was not much bigger than the bed that fit into it, but it was a palace compared to the conditions in steerage. Kristina fell asleep as soon as her cheek touched the pillow.

She dreamed of moving decks and high seas, and woke up in terror. She was relieved to find that her bed was fixed to an unmoving floor, and the walls of her room remained vertical. *I'm here, here in New York!* she said to herself. She fell asleep again, and this time she slept soundly.

In the morning Pani Melcek prepared bread and eggs for her, then prepared to leave for her own job. "Today you must walk around to learn the neighborhood so you don't get lost. Remember the house number, and don't cross any streets. Come back here for lunch and after that your mother will take you to your job."

The street downstairs was exciting but more frightening now that she was alone. Children were playing, calling, fighting. She could understand nothing of this new language being spoken around her. Around the corner, where the shops were, she stared at the signs to see if she could recognize any words. Not one. Only the numbers were the same, but what was that curious little letter, ¢? She tried

reading the words, sounding out the letters in the way they would sound in Slovak, but they made no sense to her. In front of a little shop, she peered in the door and saw a barber cutting a man's hair. On the door were signs that said: *SHAVE 5¢. HAIR CUT 5¢.* She read them to herself. *"S'hah vay. Hah eer coot."*

Another store had groceries; she painstakingly read all the printed words to see if she could recognize any of them. *MILK 5¢.* Could that be *mleko*? A little thrill of insight went through her. But she was not brave enough to test her theory. And she did not have a container to buy milk in anyway, so her thirst would have to wait.

The bakery smells entranced her again, and she stood for a while just inhaling. Other people walking down the street slowed down to better catch the aroma too, she noticed. A few of them smiled at her.

Push carts lined the rest of the street. She looked at all the colors and varieties of fruit and again tried to read the signs. *AP PLAY MAY LON, GRAH PAY . . .* they had no meaning for her. But what was that? *BA NA NA?* The funny yellow things? She was so excited, she spoke to the vendor, pointing to the sign for him to confirm her understanding.

"Ba na na?"

The vendor broke off a bunch of six bananas, and handed them to her. She was right! English was going to be possible!

But now the vendor thought she wanted to buy them. She couldn't explain that she only wanted to understand the word. She opened her neck purse and showed him the coins that remained. He shook his head. Her coins were not American. Then he shrugged his shoulders, pointed to the number *5c* on his sign and counted out five of her coins. They were all of different denominations, and amounted to quite a bit in Hungary. She could buy three salamis with that amount.

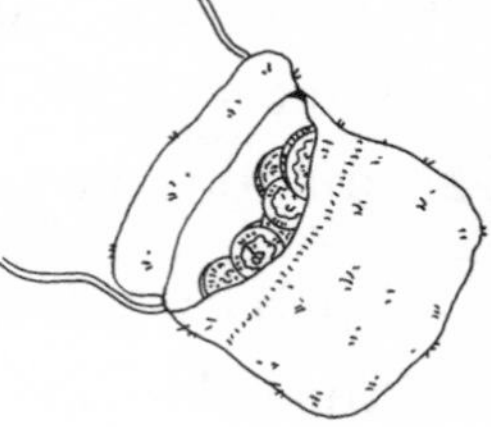

"No!" she said, and handed the bananas back. *Bananas were much too expensive!*

The vendor looked

around. There were quite a few people passing on the street, some eyeing the transaction. He grudgingly returned her coins.

"Stupid." He called after her.

So that's what Mother meant when she said people would try to cheat you when you were a greenhorn. She wondered what *stupid* meant; clearly it wasn't very nice. She practiced saying it to herself just in case someone should try to cheat her again. *Banana. Stupid. Greenhorn.* Now she knew three English words.

Chapter 7: First Job in America

"She's very small. Are you sure she's fourteen?"

"Yes, and she's a very good worker."

"It's a lot of responsibility, taking care of a baby. We expected someone much bigger."

"Kristina took care of my whole family in Slovakia."

"Well, in any case, she can start at four dollars a month."

"But you said six dollars when we spoke before."

"That's because we expected someone much bigger."

"The work will be the same."

"We'll pay four dollars. Remember she'll have a place to live, and we have to feed her, too."

Mother spoke fluent Hungarian to the family where Kristina was to begin her work in America. They were Mr. and Mrs. Zlady, who owned a dry-cleaning and tailoring shop. Kristina would take care of the baby, wash the dishes, and do any small chores the Zladys needed done.

Kristina looked with fear and dismay at the home she would be living in—three small dreary rooms on the first floor. Was this to be her home in America? The front room was where the dry-cleaning customers came, where Mr. Zlady worked all day with harsh smelling chemicals and Mrs. Zlady sewed at a foot operated machine. The center room was the kitchen, dark and gloomy; the only window looked out at a wall just a few feet away. With buildings six stories tall, not much light got down to the first floor in the narrow center space that the buildings were built around. The back room was the bedroom for the Zladys, and their year-old child, Palko. At night a folding cot would be opened up for Kristina in the kitchen. There was a smelly toilet in the hall that the family shared with three other families on the first floor. It was a truly ugly and dirty place to live compared to her bright, sun-filled home in Slovakia.

The baby Palko, though, was beautiful, with dark curly hair and very large brown eyes. Mrs. Zlady showed him to Kristina, and offered him to her. He was sleepy and cranky and didn't want to sit on Kristina's lap. He clung nervously to his mother.

After the introductions and arrangements were made, Mother had to return to her job. Kristina was now on hers. "Just take Palko outside," said Mrs. Zlady. "Let him cry there, and get tired. Then when he naps, you can learn about the kitchen chores."

It was not long before Kristina won Palko over and she enjoyed the baby and his playful ways. She loved bathing him, feeding him, changing his diapers, keeping him amused and consoling him when he was upset or cranky or hurt. The day was busy and full, and when Palko took his nap, there was tidying and dishes to do.

Kristina was eager to learn English, but she saw little chance for it, working for this Hungarian family, since they did not speak English either. They managed their business through gestures and pointing if the customers were not also Hungarian. But most were.

When Kristina was out on the street, she carefully listened to the conversations of people, and especially the children playing in the alleys. It was hard to catch on to whole sentences, but there were occasional words that she could isolate and practice to herself, even though she didn't know what they meant. She rehearsed them so she wouldn't forget them, and saved them to ask Mother when she saw her on her day off.

Palko was a fussy eater, and Kristina tried coaxing him to open his mouth for a spoonful of the cereal that she had prepared for his breakfast. She coaxed him first in Hungarian, then in Slovak, but he would not eat. Then she decided to use English. Maybe that magic language would open up the baby's lips.

"Shuh dup. Palko." she said as she offered him a spoonful. "Shuh dup. Shuh dup ..." she said sweetly.

Mrs. Zlady happened to come in at that moment from her work in the front. "What are you saying to my little Palko?"

"I thought I would speak to him in English," explained Kristina.

"Do you know what you are saying?"

"Shuh dup. I hear children saying it in the streets. I wanted to teach Palko English."

Mrs. Zlady glowered at Kristina. *"'Shut up'* means to close your mouth and be quiet. It is a very fresh and rude thing to say."

"Oh." Kristina was humiliated. She'd better not use words in English until she checked what they meant.

Although the Zladys were kind, they were not in the least rich. Not only did they pay her the lowest possible wage, but they had very little to give her to eat, and they had very little to eat themselves. Kristina was as hungry as she had been back in Slovakia, but now she had all the delicious food of America in front of her eyes everyday when she went outside, but with no money to buy it.

When Thursday came, Mother brought Kristina to Melceks, where she gobbled down the food she had hungered for all week. She told her about the small portions she received and Mother then supplied Kristina with extra bread and fruit, that she hid by day in her little folded cot. She was afraid that the Zlady's would become angry that she had more to eat than they did. She was careful to keep it in a tin box, and to wipe up any crumbs, since there were cockroaches in the apartment and she and Mrs. Zlady were often busy killing them.

In a few weeks Mother brought good news. She had found a new job for Kristina.

"You'll be working for a rich couple in a fine apartment. The lady is French and can speak German as well. Her husband speaks German and Hungarian, and his English is very good. He has promised to teach you English, and you will earn nine dollars a month."

More than double what she was getting now! And she would have her own room. It sounded like heaven.

Mr. Neuman was much older than Father, and much better fed! He was tall and fat, with silvery hair and a round, soft, kindly face. He spoke in a soft voice and it seemed everything about him was soft and gentle.

Mrs. Neuman, his wife, was also tall, but slender, and with long blond curls. She was the most beautiful woman Kristina had ever seen. She was much younger than her husband, and had a royal air about her. Kristina was proud to be working for such an elegant mistress.

The apartment was spacious; there was a dining room as well as a kitchen, and a huge parlor for entertaining guests. Kristina's jaw dropped when she saw her very own room, with a door and a lock on the inside. It was something she had never imagined in her life, a retreat where no one could enter unless she allowed them to. It contained a small bed, a little chest of drawers and a mirror. A mirror all her own. She wondered if some day she would ever have enough possessions to fill up the empty drawers.

In the evening, a buzzer rang in the kitchen. Where was it coming from? Mrs. Neuman opened a little door in the wall and showed her the dumbwaiter. Mrs. Neuman put bags of garbage on the dumb-waiter shelf, then called something down the shaft, and the contraption lowered itself out of sight, showing a set of ropes, some moving up and some moving down. *What in the world was it? How was it moving?*

Mrs. Neuman spoke to her husband in German, and Mr. Neuman spoke to Kristina in Hungarian. Each morning he explained the various chores that his wife wanted done, so in this way communication of a sort went on, added to by Mrs. Neuman's use of gestures and demonstrations. Misunderstandings that couldn't be resolved in the daytime had to wait until evening to be straightened out. He also taught her a few sentences in English, but he didn't have time to really make sure she understood or could say them. She remembered only the first three numbers in English: *wun too tree.*

One day during the first week, Mrs. Neuman was out of the house when the dumbwaiter buzzer rang. Kristina opened the door, placed two bags of garbage on the shelf, and closed the door. She did not remember that she must say something to the superintendant who was waiting below to know when she had finished so he could pull the ropes that moved the dumbwaiter down to the floor below.

The buzzer rang again, long and loud. She opened the door. She could hear a man's voice downstairs yelling something up at her. What did he want? She closed the door again. The buzzer sounded and did not stop. She opened the door and yelled down the only English words she knew.

"Shut up stupid banana! Shut up!"

The yells from below became violently angry. Kristina slammed the door shut. *What if the owner of that angry voice should come upstairs to punish her! She was terrified. What had she done?* She ran to her room and locked the door behind her then slid herself under to bed to hide.

It was not long before the doorbell rang. Kristina hoped that, if she did not make a sound, he would think that she was not there and would go away. But the bell rang and rang, and Kristina's heart pounded in fear. *Would he break down the door? Could he really want to harm her for her rudeness? Oh why had she said those words, when Mrs. Zlady had told her that it was rude?*

Finally, the bell stopped, and Kristina held her breath fearing it would begin again. She did not move from under the bed. After about five minutes, she heard a key in the lock, and the door opened. Of course, the super would have a key! Would he find her?

"Kristina! Where are you?"

It was Mrs. Neuman.

Very cautiously Kristina wriggled out from under the bed, and came out. Mrs. Neuman's eyes were blazing with anger, and there standing out in the hall was a dark, strong-looking man with a big ring of keys in his hand. Kristina dove back into her room and locked the door. She did not come out until she heard footsteps going to the door and the door close behind them.

It was up to Mr. Neuman to find out why Kristina had refused to open the door when Mrs. Neuman had gone out without her key. He instructed Kristina in how to apologize in English, both to his wife and to the super. He explained that after putting the garbage on the dumbwaiter, she should have called down, "Ready." Or "All right."

Mr. Neuman told her that they were going to entertain some important friends the next evening, so Kristina would have a busy day. She was to wear a maid's serving uniform, which he presented her with. It was left over from their last maid, and was far too large for Kristina's small frame. He gave her a needle and thread, and she sewed it to a better size for herself. She tried it on

and was quite pleased with her appearance.

The next morning Kristina followed Mrs. Neuman to the pushcarts and the butcher shop, staying quietly in the background. A six-pound roast from the butcher's, four pounds of potatoes, a pound of string beans, and a quart of berries from the pushcarts. Bread, butter, sugar, milk, and cream from the grocer's. It was Kristina's job to carry the bundles home. She was to walk three steps behind her mistress. As the bundles accumulated with each purchase, the load became heavier and heavier. Kristina had a hard time keeping up with the fast pace and was constantly shifting the bundles to redistribute the weight. Her back and neck muscles ached, and her fingers became numb. Men stared in their direction, and at first Kristina thought they were looking at her. Then she realized it was the tall, beautiful Mrs. Neuman who commanded their attention. Mrs. Neuman walked like a princess, with her blonde curly head held high and her long legs taking gentle strides, block after block.

Back at the apartment, Mrs. Neuman showed her, through gestures and some broken Hungarian, how to clean the house. Then she had Kristina peel potatoes, chop the vegetables, wash and trim a box full of luscious red strawberries, and set the table. She whipped a bowl of cream and watched as Mrs. Neuman created an artistic masterpiece of strawberries, cream, and cake. *Would there be any of this feast for her?*

In the evening when the guests arrived, she took their coats as Mr. Neuman had instructed her, and hung them up in the hall closet.

How her mouth watered as she served the juicy roast beef, baked potatoes, carrots and gravy to the Neumans and their guests in the dining room. Her

lunch of bread and cheese seemed to have been so long ago. She listened to the growling noises in her stomach with embarrassment. Back in the kitchen, she washed the pots and cooking pans while the guests were eating, and finally, Mrs. Neuman rang the little silver bell to signal Kristina to come in and clear the dishes from the table. She carefully reached around the left of each guest as she had been taught, quietly, so as not to interrupt their conversation.

Kristina saw with delight that a few of the guests had left slices of meat on their plates. She quickly picked them up with her fingers and popped them into her mouth without stopping in her trip back to the kitchen.

Mrs. Neuman jumped up, shouting sharp words and charged into the kitchen after her. What had she done wrong?

Her mistress' eyes blazed with fury. She slapped Kristina across the face, and grabbed the dishes from her hands. She scolded and screamed, but Kristina could not understand a word. Then Mrs. Neuman pointed first toward Kristina's room and then toward the front door. Kristina was being fired! At her new job less than a week and she was being fired!

Mr. Neuman came into the kitchen, calmly spoke to his wife in German, then spoke to Kristina in Hungarian.

"Why did you eat the meat on the dishes in front of all the guests?"

"Because I was hungry."

"You are supposed to wait until you have finished for the day before you eat your meal."

"I couldn't help myself. I was very hungry. I didn't know I wasn't supposed to eat it. They left it on their plates, so I knew they didn't want it."

"It was very rude. Mrs. Neuman is very embarrassed that you did that in front of our guests."

Mrs. Neuman broke in again, still angry, pointing toward the door. Her husband calmed her, and spoke again with Kristina.

"Do you want to keep working here, Kristina?"

What other choice was there? It had taken Mother weeks to get her this job. "Yes, sir."

"Then you must never do what you did again."

"No, sir."

"Now, dry your eyes and serve the dessert. You may eat your supper before you do the dishes," said Mr. Neuman.

"Thank you, sir."

Kristina had lost all hope about the strawberry cream cake and she served it as if she were totally oblivious to it. And the guests did what she would have done, cleaned the plates thoroughly, and she dared not even lick the few remaining smears of cream when she cleared the table.

She decided it would be better to have the

work done before she ate, now that the meat had taken the edge off her hunger. She dutifully cleared the kitchen and washed the dishes. Then at last she sat down at the kitchen table and, listening to the lively chatter in the dining room, she ate her supper of bread and cheese.

Chapter 8: Bananas

On another evening, Mr. Neuman told her in Hungarian, "There will be guests tomorrow evening. You will stay here tomorrow and clean the house while Mrs. Neuman goes out shopping. A delivery boy will bring the groceries and send them up in the dumbwaiter."

"Yes, sir."

"Just take the bag out and put the groceries away, in the ice box, or cabinet, wherever they belong. Put the fruit in the large crystal bowl and arrange it nicely, and set it on the dining room table."

"Yes, sir."

"Mrs. Neuman will go from the market to her hairdresser. She will be back by four o'clock to start cooking. Be sure the house is completely cleaned, and the silverware polished. These are very important guests. We want to make a good impression."

No food was left in the house, so Kristina was to wait to eat breakfast of cheese and bread when the groceries were delivered. Around noon, when Mrs. Neuman had been gone for about an hour, the kitchen buzzer rang and Kristina opened the little dumbwaiter door to find the large bag of groceries that had been hauled up by the delivery boy. She took in the bag, called "All right," in English so the boy would lower the dumbwaiter. Then she closed the little door. She was ravenously hungry, and looking forward to a good sandwich of bread and cheese.

The first thing she took out of the bag was a bunch of small yellow bananas.

Kristina's hunger and curiosity made her careless. Pan Melcek had told her that someday she would like bananas, and Kristina was certain that she had acted like a greenhorn in not being willing to taste them before. She resolved that this was her chance. If she wanted to become American, she must try to like everything American that Americans liked. Mrs. Neuman would probably not miss one banana.

Kristina plucked the smallest banana off the bunch and carefully peeled it as she had seen Pan Melcek do. She broke off a small piece and popped it into her mouth, expecting it to taste like a potato or some plain vegetable. As she chewed, she marveled at the amazing delicate texture, the firm substance becoming soft and unresisting. Slowly the sweetness of the banana blossomed in her mouth, exciting her taste buds. It was delicious! She bit off another piece, and another, and the banana was gone.

Kristina put the milk and butter into the ice box, the bread into the bread box, the cans of food into the cupboards near the sink. There were grapes, oranges, apples, and the bananas for the fruit bowl. She got a large glass bowl, and as she placed the fruit in it, changing the positions of each in an attempt to balance the colors and the shapes, her mouth continued watering, and on impulse, she broke another banana off the bunch and quickly ate it. It was as sweet and satisfying as the first had been. Before she knew it, she had eaten a third one. Bananas were wonderful! A fourth banana found its way into her mouth. Only two bananas were left, and they looked conspicuously lonely among the apples and the grapes.

And then Kristina came to her senses. *What had she done! Mrs. Neuman would be furious. She would surely be fired this time. What could she do?*

She must go out to the fruit vendors and buy bananas with her own money to replace them. She resolved to do that immediately. It wouldn't take very long, and she could finish cleaning the kitchen as soon as she returned. And as long as she was going to buy more bananas, she might as well eat one more.

She peeled the fifth banana, and carefully wrapped all of the peels in newspaper before throwing them in the garbage. She then got her house key out of the top drawer of the dresser in her little room, stepped out into the hall, locked the door and put the key into her purse. It was the first time she was going out of the house alone, but she had already accompanied Mrs. Neuman on four shopping trips, so she felt that she could find the street with the pushcarts and fruit vendors with no trouble.

She crossed the street, being careful to watch her step for the ever-present horse droppings. One of those crazy auto-things clattered and banged down the cross street under the el. Kristina had the last banana with her, peeled, but she didn't feel very hungry for it. She had never thrown food away in her life, so she slowly ate it as she walked two blocks, turned right around a corner, and walked another block. This route brought her to the market street lined with vendors, pushcarts, and hundreds of shoppers, just as she remembered. Her stomach was beginning to feel uncomfortable, making churning noises, and she was sorry she had eaten the last banana.

She went up to the first pushcart at the corner. It was stocked with apples, oranges and plenty of

bananas, but Kristina was surprised to see that they were mostly green. The next cart had large yellow bananas, but no small ones to match the ones she had eaten. The third pushcart had small bananas, but they were too ripe, with brown speckles and lines on the skins. It wasn't as simple as Kristina had thought. But there were plenty of carts; the street was lined with them for many blocks in each direction. She would just have to look until she found a bunch of small, perfectly yellow bananas that matched the ones Mrs. Neuman had bought. But every time she looked at bananas, her stomach churned and seemed to turn over again. Kristina wove her way down the line of pushcarts, checked the bananas at each one, crossed the street, and finally found a pushcart that had just the right kind of bananas—small and yellow. She took five cents out of her purse to pay the vendor, and quickly headed for home.

She turned and walked down the pushcart-lined street, rounded the corner, and walked a block to the next street. She paused. Was it right or left she was supposed to go? Or was she supposed to walk two blocks before she turned? The tall, six-story buildings all looked pretty much the same, and she didn't recognize any specific landmarks. Why hadn't she counted the blocks she had walked among the pushcarts while she was looking for bananas? She walked another block and turned left. She knew that above the entranceway to her building the letters *O-N-E* were written. If the streets had names in America, then her building must have a name, too. She pronounced the letters as she would in Slovak. *"Onay."*

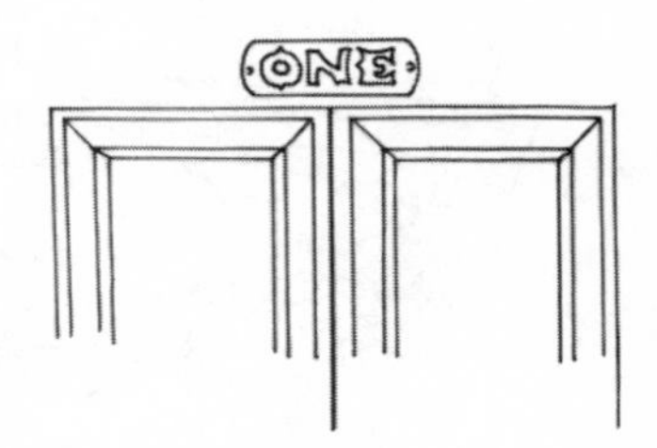

A woman with two small children in tow was coming down the street toward her.

"Pardon, Madam," she said politely. *"Onay?"*

"Excuse me?" said the woman.

"Onay?" Kristina pointed at the closest building to indicate that she was looking for a building with that name, but the woman did not understand.

By this time, Kristina's stomach was churning badly. The taste of digesting bananas came up her throat in small belches, and made her wish she would never see a banana again. She decided to go back to the market street where the pushcarts were, and start again; surely it would be clear when she got there.

But the street with the pushcarts was lined with vendors for blocks and blocks in both directions. They all looked alike, just as the buildings all looked alike.

A large clock on one building chimed the hour. It was two o'clock! She had to get home and finish cleaning the house before Mrs. Neuman got there! With or without bananas, if the house was not scrupulously clean for this evening's company, she was in danger of being fired. Her mother would be furious if she lost this job after only three weeks.

Now she was in pain from her stomach contractions. Tears filled her eyes; she started to wander blindly up and down the streets before she got hold of herself and made a plan. *I must do this carefully. Go up three blocks, turn right, walk down three blocks, turn right.. Even if I have to walk over this entire city, I will find my building! I'll ask everyone I meet; surely someone will understand me!*

She walked up to each person who passed her in the street, asking, "*Onay*?" Some people brushed right by her without stopping; others stopped, sympathetic, puzzled over the meaning of her question for a while, and then, unable to assist her, shrugged their shoulders and walked on. At last she saw a postman delivering the afternoon mail. He of all people should know the names of the houses!

It hurt to move fast because of the growing gasses in her stomach, but she hurried after him as best she could. "Onay?" she asked, full of hope.

He, too, shook his head in bewilderment. She couldn't believe it.

A clock in the distance was striking three. The postman looked at her tear-filled eyes and the desperate look on her face and produced a pencil from his large leather sack. He found a large white envelope and gestured to her to write on it. She drew the front entrance way of her house, the broad double doors with the large letters, O - N - E written above them.

"*Onay*," said Kristina, pointing to the letters.

"No," he said firmly and tapped her letters with the pencil. "Wun."

"Wun?"

"Yes. Wun." He wrote an equal sign next to the letters and the number 'one' after that.

"Wun too tree?"

The postman nodded and smiled. "Yes. One two three."

Well, why didn't they spell it W-U-N, wondered Kristina. Why did they spell *wun* like *onay*?

The postman led her around the corner and pointed up the block. Yes, indeed, that looked like the right street. She bowed and repeated in English, "Tank you, tank you!," and then hurried to her building.

When she reached the fourth floor apartment, out of breath, stomach aching, there was only one thing she wanted to do: lie down and let her poor churning stomach rest. But a glance at the wall clock in the kitchen showed it was already three fifteen. She had just forty-five minutes to make the beds, wash the dishes, sweep the floors, dust the furniture, polish the silverware, and wax the tables! She quickly arranged the new bananas, now nauseating to her, in the fruit bowl, and with fear driving her, ignored the pain in her stomach, and flew about the house. By four o'clock, all the chores were done and the apartment sparkled. Kristina was polishing the last few pieces of silver when Mrs. Neuman's ring at the doorbell came. Sweat glistened on Kristina's brow. The bananas had been replaced, the house was cleaned, and the peels were safely wrapped up in the garbage. Was there any way for her employer to discover what had happened today?

Mrs. Neuman made her usual inspection, checking all the rooms, looking under the beds for dust, running her finger on top of the mantelpiece. She smiled when she found no dust clinging to her finger.

But then she went to the dining room table. Kristina pretended to be looking at the spoon she was shining, but glanced up to watch Mrs. Neuman's inspection of the crystal fruit bowl. Kristina's stomach cramped, and she almost doubled over with the pain. Could Mrs. Neuman tell that those were not the same bananas she had bought this morning? Could she hear the awful churning in Kristina's stomach?

Mrs. Neuman picked up the bananas and turned them around, examining them. Kristina's mouth was dry, and a lump began to form in her throat. She was found out!

"Iss very gut, Kristina," said Mrs. Neuman. She twisted the largest banana off the bunch. She held it out to Kristina and smiled. "I am happy. Gut job. Here, take banana."

Chapter 9: Central Park

At last Thursday came. The whole day off. Mother arrived early to take Kristina with her. Kristina hugged her as though she hadn't seen her for months instead of just this one week. How good it was to see Mother.

As they rode the el to the Melcek's, Kristina told her mother the incident she'd had with the super and the dumbwaiter, and the horror of getting lost. Somehow, the things that had seemed so frightening and embarrassing now came out as very funny stories in the safety of Mother's warm presence.

"You will have to learn English as soon as possible."

"It's so hard, Mother. People talk so fast.

Mr. Neuman doesn't have much time. And the spelling doesn't say what the sounds say. I don't think I can ever learn."

"If two-year old babies learn to speak English, you can, too. Today we will take a tour of the city, and I will teach you to read the street signs. You are now in the greatest city in the world, did you know that?

"Really?" asked Kristina.

"Three and a half million people live here."

How many of that three and a half million were Slovak? wondered Kristina, as they climbed the final flight of stairs to get to the Melceks' apartment. She felt a special comfort there with her own townspeople. The smiles and greetings and warmth of speaking to friends in her own language was a great relief after speaking Hungarian with Mr. Neuman, and struggling with English all week.

"It's good to speak Slovak after hearing only strange sounds for seven days," she said. "It feels like an escape from a mental jail."

They had bought cheese and fruit at a grocer's below, and took some of Pan Melcek's freshly baked bread to make a picnic lunch. Thursday was the maid's day off: Mother and Kristina and four friends were all going to Central Park!

Central Park was a fairyland of splendid carriages, beautiful women dressed in long, fancy-laced dresses, wearing wide-brimmed hats topped with flowers and fruit. There were bridal paths with men and women in riding costumes, cantering gracefully on fine horses. The group of friends walked over smooth green lawns, through shady groves, past vine-covered arbors and huge gray rocks. They saw statues of famous men from many nations,

and watched men playing cricket in a large field.

Glorious sounds came from a distance, and Kristina was delighted to see a huge rotating building, with magnificent horses, tigers and giraffes rising up and down on poles, filled with children.

"It's a carousel," said Mother. Would you like to ride? It will cost you five cents."

Kristina thought of what five cents would buy. A loaf of bread. A quart of milk. A ride on this magnificent musical zoo, on a horse that rose up and down seemed like the greatest thing a five cent piece could ever buy. "Oh yes, yes. I want to ride that horse right there." She pointed to a handsome black horse with painted jewels in his harness. They all bought tickets and rode, Kristina delighting in her ups and downs, with the beat of the calliope thundering through the carousel and her whole body. Afterwards they ate their picnic lunch and watched others ride.

Next, the menagerie.

What animals! Kristina gaped as she saw the awesome elephant in action, waving his trunk around at the people, begging for peanuts, fanning his enormous ears, and rolling his little eyes. How did anything so massive ever get to exist? She could not imagine such an animal; there was not one even in her fairy tale book.

Near the menagerie was Fifth Avenue. The houses were all like castles. "This is Millionaire's Row," said Mother. Each mansion was huge and wildly different from the one next to it. One had dozens of turrets, the next had lavish carvings and gargoyles; there were stone, brick, marble, and mosaic fronts in a bewildering assortment.

"The families who live here are richer even than King Franz-Josef of Hungary," said Mother. She even knew the names of some: the Vanderbilts, the Astors,

the Rockefellers, the Whitneys. Kristina watched the elegantly uniformed servants coming from back entrances of the house, carrying baskets, doing errands. *What must it be like to work in palaces like these?*

That night, as she lay in bed, a wonderful plan was beginning to take shape in her mind. With her new higher wages, she would be able to help Mother save money so that in one year, Anna could come, and with the three of them working, they would be able to bring another sister each year, until all of her sisters were in America. Then Father could make his choice of coming or not coming. But Mother and Anna, Betka, Olga, and Susanna would all be in New York, working, eating well, and seeing each other on Thursdays and Sundays. They would be a happy family at last, all together in the same city. It was such a wonderful dream. Maybe they could even find a rich family that needed a cook and had a lot of rooms to clean or children to take care of and Kristina and her mother and sisters would all work in the same house and see each other every day. Maybe, it could even be in one of those magnificent palaces she had seen today on Fifth Avenue!

It was a wonderful dream and with it, she put herself peacefully to sleep.

Chapter 10: Alone in America

It was autumn, and as was now usual on Thursdays, Kristina stepped sprightly up the stairs to the Melceks. *Ah, it would be good to see Mother.* There were so many stories to tell her of her week's learnings, her aching back, her embarrassment in the butcher shop, and especially Mr. Neuman's new car. She had been looking forward excitedly to the trip to Coney Island that Mother had promised they would all go to.

By the fifth landing, Kristina was a bit out of breath, and waited patiently for Pani Melcek to respond to the knock on the door. "Your mother is not here yet, Kristina," Pani Melcek told her as she invited her to sit down.

Kristina immediately started to worry. Mother had always arrived ahead of her. Where could she be?

"Wait, it's very early. There are so many little things that can delay a person," said Pani Melcek. "Here, help yourself to some coffee."

But an hour later, Kristina was half mad with worry. When Mother finally arrived, her face was pale. Mother did not look like herself. She was not walking strong and tall as she usually did.

"What is it, Mother?"

"A letter has come," said Mother with almost no energy in her voice. "From your father. It's bad news . . . ."

"What's wrong? Is Susanna sick? Or . . ." Kristina felt the blood run out of her head. She held onto the wall. She remembered holding little Milka in her arms as she was struggling against the terrible fever.

"No. It's not Susanna."

"Anna? Betka? Olga?"

"No, not your sisters. It's your father. He has fallen and broken his hip."

Kristina felt immediate relief that it was not her sisters who were ailing. But her mother's next words were like a punch to her stomach.

"I will have to go back to Myjava," her mother said, almost in a whisper.

The words hit Kristina and she instantly went deaf to them. It could not be. *Mother could not be saying these impossible words.*

"Why?" Kristina choked. "Anna can take care of Father. He will be better by the time you get there. The letter must be a month old already. When Betka had a broken ankle from falling out of the attic window, she was walking in six weeks."

"This is different, Kristina. He fell from a wagon when a horse was frightened and running wild. His hip was broken in many places. The doctor thinks your father may never walk again. I must go home."

Strangling emotions coursed through Kristina. How could her father be so cruel to her again when she had gotten so far away from his strap? How could he take her mother away from her? She could never stay in America if her mother was not there.

"What about me?"

"You will be OK. The Melceks will be your guardians when you have a problem. You have a roof over your head and regular meals. You have nothing to worry about here. You are in America. Everything will be alright."

How could Mother be so wrong. Nothing would be right. Kristina struggled with herself to stay calm, but emotions overcame her.

"I hate America! There is nothing here that I want. I eat only scraps from the table. Mrs. Neuman is mean and selfish and always angry at me. The work is very hard. I miss my sisters. And learning English is impossible!"

"You have a job and you are earning money. Our family needs your pay to live."

"Nine dollars a month is nothing! I will be broken down under Mrs. Neuman's bundles and starved by her stinginess, and cheated by everyone around me because I can't speak English. If you are going back to Myjava, I have to go, too."

"No, Kristina."

"I can't stay here. There is nothing for me here! The only good thing about America is that I can see you on my days off—otherwise America is a crazy, noisy, stinking, dangerous place to be."

"Kristina, you are not a baby. You are almost grown. You can not cling to your mother all your life."

Kristina's tears flowed profusely, and deep wracking pain gripped her sobbing body. "You've been gone almost all my life. First to Vienna, then to America. I came here to be with you."

"And I brought you here to have a better life than you could have in Myjava."

"It is not better without you. I am going with you."

"There is no money for that!"

Kristina could not believe she was saying the words that were plummeting out of her mouth. "There is. There is enough for two tickets! We have saved eighty dollars. You told me."

"Father will need a doctor. We will need to eat. This is reality."

"You only love Father! You've never loved me!" *All of her sister Anna's words seemed so true now.* "You never loved any of us. You wouldn't have left us."

"Didn't I also leave Father?" pleaded Mother. "Do you forget so quickly what it is like to be hungry? I have a trade—I am a cook. I can sell my work for money, but only where people can afford to pay. In Vienna or America, there are people who can afford a servant. Not in Myjava. I had to leave my husband and my children in order to keep you alive! Do you understand that my heart was broken?"

Kristina felt dark clouds raging in her mind. "You had ten children and five are dead! I wish I was one of the dead!"

"Kristina! Don't say that!"

Mother collapsed in tears of frustration, hurt

and powerlessness. "Come, let me hold you!"

"I hate you!" Kristina was completely out of control of herself, and did not know what she was saying. It was as though she had to do anything to make the truth go away.

"I am your mother!"

"If you are my mother, don't go! Don't go! Don't leave me again!" Kristina screamed. Then she screamed longer and louder. She lost control and the screaming began to take on its own life. Her throat opened and large gulps of bottomless pain transformed into sound, taxing her chest, her throat, her lungs. She would have to scream forever, for the pain would not stop.

"She's gone crazy!" Mother went to the sink and filled a basin of water. She carried it, helpless to stop Kristina in any other way. She got ready to throw it at Kristina. That would bring her to her senses.

"No, leave her," said Melcek who was standing in the next room during all of this. "This hurts. Let her get it all out. She'll be OK. We are going to care for her."

After a long time, the raging energy spent itself. Kristina could cry no more, could feel no more. She sniffled and sobbed in exhaustion, and slowly regained control of herself. She was able to see that at the height of the pain, when she had screamed the loudest, raged the worst, she had not been herself, 14-year-old Kristina, but a long ago Kristina, the seven-year-old, whose mother had left for the first time to go off to Vienna. A seven-year old who could not bear to lose her mother, who could not see a future reunion, who could not bear to wait. A seven-year-old, two years older than little Susanna. Kristina remembered Susanna's death grip around her waist when she had left.

Susanna was the one who needed mother. Even more than father did. Kristina was fourteen, she had survived, and she would survive now on her own. She could let go of her need for her mother for the sake of little Susanna, her little treasure.

"I'm sorry, Mother," she said in a voice that she was not sure was her own, deep and unrecognizable .

"Life is not easy, Kristina. We must do what we must do."

Kristina's body was heavy and limp. There wasn't an ounce of force left in it. She could only sleep.

She awoke late in the afternoon. Mother was gone. There was a note.

"I am going to the steamship company to get my ticket. There is a ship next Wednesday."

That would be Kristina's birthday. Her fifteenth birthday.

The day came, and Mrs. Neuman grudgingly gave Kristina the morning off to accompany her mother to the Hudson piers to say goodbye. In exchange, Kristina had agreed to work all of Sunday.

Kristina waved her handkerchief as the huge ship was slowly inched out of its berth by the harbor tugs. She waved until the return waving of her Mother was indistinguishable from all the other masses of hands and handkerchiefs on the lower deck of the *Kaiser Wilhelm der Grosse*. Kristina was now alone in America. Fifteen, and the sole provider for her parents and four sisters.

She wiped the tears from her eyes and began the long walk to the el. As she passed a corner store, she suddenly turned. She saw something out of the corner of her eye that struck her like lightning.

It was a book, posed in the store window, one of many books. But the title made it the most wonderful book in the world. *"Anglictina pre Slovakov.*—English for Slovaks." She went in and asked the price. Eighty-five cents. Two days' pay. A fortune. But it was a key. A key to open doors in America. She bought it.

With the book under her arm, she felt an energy

flow to her mind, her heart, her whole body. Her legs walked easier; she was lighter. She was almost flying. She would not have to wait for Mr. Neuman to have time to teach her. She would not have to be embarrassed about forgetting his lessons. A book was patient. She could read the explanations over and over, as many times as she wanted to without worrying that it would become angry or think she was slow. She could study it until she understood it.

On the el, she opened to the first page and read it:

"Vitajte v Amerike!

Welcome to America!"